WESTFIELD PUBLIC L
333 West Hoover S
Westfield, IN 46074

P9-DEY-510

Discarded by
Westfield Washington
Public Library

alchemy

alchemy

MARGARET MAHY

MARGARET K. MCELDERRY BOOKS
New York London Toronto Sydney Singapore

MARGARET K. MCELDERRY BOOKS
An imprint of Simon & Schuster Children's Publishing Division
1230 Avenue of the Americas, New York, New York 10020

This book is a work of fiction. Any references to historical events, real people, or real locales are used fictitiously. Other names, characters, places, and incidents are products of the author's imagination, and any resemblance to actual events or locales or persons, living or dead, is entirely coincidental.

Copyright © 2003 by Margaret Mahy

All rights reserved, including the right
of reproduction in whole or in part in any form.

Book design by Ann Sullivan
The text for this book is set in Aldine 401 BT.

Printed in the United States of America
10 9 8 7 6 5 4 3 2 1

Library of Congress Cataloging-in-Publication Data
Mahy, Margaret.
Alchemy / Margaret Mahy.
p. cm.
Summary: Seventeen-year-old Roland discovers that an unpopular girl in his school is studying alchemy and finds that their destiny is linked with that of a power-hungry magician.
ISBN 0-689-85053-0
[1. Alchemy—Fiction. 2. Magic—Fiction. 3. Magicians—Fiction.] I. Title.
PZ7.M2773 Aj 2003
[Fic]—dc21
2002005973

ALSO BY MARGARET MAHY

24 Hours
Memory
The Tricksters
The Catalogue of the Universe
The Changeover
The Haunting

(Margaret K. McElderry Books)

TO PATRICIA—
always thinking of you!

alchemy

DREAMING

So here it was again . . . coming through the dark at him—the dream, the nightmare that had haunted him for years. OK, he'd been through it all before. He already knew what was in store. He already knew there was no way of waking out of this particular dream until it had run its course. It would end in terror—as it always did. And yet that terror seemed to be *necessary*. He felt himself dividing like a cell, becoming two, then three, people—the dreamer, the child in the dream, and someone outside it—watching the dreamer dream . . . watching the child move innocently toward the coffin . . . and feeling the familiar panic as he watched it happening yet again.

Look! There they go, moving through the fairground, side by side, Roland and his father—hand in hand, yet apparently joined in other ways as well. And in spite of the reassuring way his father's hand curls around his fingers, Roland the watcher knows that Roland the dream child is becoming more and more alarmed with every step. He is being warned . . . warned from inside. I'm frightened, *he is thinking.* I am going to change. Everything is going to change. There's no escape. Here it comes!

Yet there is not one single frightening thing to be seen in the world around him. There is nothing he can reasonably shrink from. Hand in hand with his father, the child walks forward.

I've been here before, *he finds himself thinking—finds himself* knowing—*as they idle along through the fair. People in the jostling crowd point things out, waving hot dogs or ice-cream cones or balloons as they do so. Looking at the bright, bobbing shapes against the yellow green of new spring leaves, Roland thinks,* There they are again, *and walks on beside his father—that very father who will disappear on the day that Roland's youngest brother, Martin, is born.* (How can I possibly know that? *Roland is wondering.* Look! That's me walking along! I'm only about four years old. Martin won't be born for years.)

Standing on the edge of a small circle of lawn, the man and his son listen as a girl sings a folk song. Then they watch a juggler juggle and an acrobat flop and flip. And now, through the applauding crowd, comes a figure enveloped in a black cloak, with a black crown on his head, and pushing a long black box in front of him.

Beneath his black crown this man is wearing a wig of black braids that frames a face so thickly covered with white paint that it seems almost featureless. It is easy to believe there is no face at all under all that blank whiteness. Roland finds he is imagining that this man might be young and handsome . . . perhaps because of his eyes, which cannot be painted out. There they are—ginger brown in color, sharp and lively, dancing within the still mask. Two helpers advance, shaking out a banner and holding it high in the air.

The magician turns to face his audience. His eyes slide over Roland, then shift to his father. And here they pause. The magician's gaze sweeps around the attentive circle. "I am Quando the Magician," he cries, his mouth a black gap in his face. Then his gaze comes back to Roland's father and hesitates before focusing on Roland once more. And from then on it seems as if everything that is said is directed at Roland alone. "I work enchantments," Quando is telling him, "but—never forget—it is also my job to trick you. And it is your job to work out just where the trick leaves off and the true magic begins." Someone carries a small table set with cards and boxes and brightly colored scarves onto the lawn beside him. The show begins.

"Where did it go? Where did it come from? How did he do that?" Roland cries. "Magic? Is it magic?"

"Trickery," his father replies, grinning as he speaks. "It's trickery. Fun, though! Fabuloso!" "Fabuloso" was something he often said when he was taken by surprise. "That's enough! Let's move on. How about some ice cream?"

Roland is enjoying the show, but he likes the idea of ice cream even more. The trick they are watching ends triumphantly. Hand in hand, they go on their way.

"You!" Quando cries. He is pointing at them commandingly. "One moment, sir! Yes, you, sir! You're longing for adventure! Don't deny it! I know you are."

"Me?" Roland's father replies, startled at being singled out in this way. "No, I'm all for a quiet life!"

Magician and man stare at each other. Then, once again, Quando's gaze drops to Roland.

"Well, what about your little boy, sir? He looks adventurous. Let's ask him." And he sinks onto his haunches in front of Roland. "You'd like an adventure, wouldn't you?" he asks playfully.

Roland understands that the magician is not playing. Nor does he fancy an adventure without knowing, beforehand, more or less what sort of an adventure it is going to be. But he does like the thought of being part of a magic trick. Besides, he is always anxious to impress his father with his cleverness and courage. He grins and nods his head.

At first his father seems to be holding him back. Roland can feel the fingers around his own fingers tightening . . . tightening until the grip is actually painful. But then they relax, and, laughing a little, his father pushes him forward. (He is being betrayed!)

"All right . . . go on, then!" his father says. "Rites of passage!"

Quando is opening the lid of the long box. "You're not scared, are you? No! Not a brave boy like you!" He asks a question, then answers it before Roland can reply himself.

"Brave! Yes, I'll be brave!"

Who said that? Not Quando, because Quando is still talking. "You're going to amaze everyone. Won't that be fun?"

Roland glances at his father, who is nodding and smiling on the edge of the crowd. Then Quando helps him climb a short blue step-ladder, lifts him, and settles him in the box (the coffin). It is padded inside and quite cozy. (How can a coffin be cozy? And how do I know it's a coffin? Does any kid of four or so recognize a coffin when he sees one?) *Quando adjusts the box on its trolley, tilting it so that Roland can look at the crowd, and the crowd can look at Roland. Then the lid (its inner surface black . . . black . . . black) closes over him. Outside in the sunny fairground someone—Quando! It must be Quando!—knocks three times on the closed lid. The sound rings in the embracing darkness, twisting through the tunnels of Roland's ears and spiraling into the very center of his head. The wooden walls around him vanish. He has lost himself.*

Suddenly, he is suspended in a space that falls away beneath him and yet somehow embraces him too. Roland blinks. Those distant grains of light are really suns. He blinks again, and silence shivers through him. It is all around him, yet he feels it deep inside his head like a song he has not yet sung aloud. He has still to find the best words for it. There is no feeling of rising or falling. In this endless space Roland feels he is both a grain of dust and a great, flaring sun. He has found himself.

The lid of the long box opens. Sunlight bursts in on him, making him blink, while the people out there peer at him, smiling, clapping, and exclaiming. Quando bows, then gestures at Roland as if he himself had just invented the boy. Smiling, he helps him to sit up again. Roland is, for some reason, anxious to stand up on his own, but Quando catches his shoulders in an unexpectedly hard grip and holds him still, looking sharply into his eyes. Their faces are only inches apart.

"Where were you?" Quando asks in a low voice. "You disappeared. Where did you go? What did you see?"

But then a new voice cuts in. That voice, heard for the first time, seems to come from deep inside Roland's own head, warning him and giving him urgent instructions.

Shhhh! *it says, like a small wave breaking on an endless shore.* Shhh! Say nothing! Don't let on!

And now something else floods through Roland—mischief, perhaps, or his own sort of secret greed. Those moments spent hanging in space, with no beginning and no ending, are going to be his alone.

"It was dark," he says, looking innocently into Quando's ginger-colored eyes. "I was shut in, but I wasn't frightened."

Quando blinks, but his expression does not change. All the same, he expresses something very like relief as he straightens, laughs, then turns toward Roland's father, who is waiting a step or two behind them.

"So! Well! Thank you for trusting me with your little treasure, sir," he cries. "Of course, he does have the gift, doesn't he? Not many people would recognize it." And Roland feels their glances lock somewhere above his head.

"A gift?" his father repeats. He laughs awkwardly. "We can always be grateful for a gift, can't we?" Quando laughs too.

"Someday he may be as talented as I am," says Quando. And he gives Roland a little parcel wrapped in silver paper, so that Roland knows he really does have a gift.

Then Roland's father picks up his son and carries him off through the fair.

"What happened to you in that box?" he asks. "Quando took the box to pieces in front of us, but you weren't there."

"I was turned into a star," Roland boasts.

"You were a star, all right," his father replies heartily, but Roland has the odd feeling that his father is talking about something different. They sit down under an oak tree and Roland opens the silver parcel, which holds six colored felt pens, a little coloring book, and a bar of chocolate. And it is now—now, when everything is over, after he has negotiated the coffin and listened to that inner voice speaking from deep inside his own head—it is now that fear strikes at him. . . . He is being changed! *He is being* told *something that he doesn't want to hear. And he can't block his ears because it is being said from deep inside him . . . said . . . said . . . said. An endless word going on and on. Roland has to break it down into short, repeated exclamations in order to understand!* Yes! *it is saying.* Yes! *Over and over again. Then,* Up! Up! Up! *And, almost immediately, that other inner voice speaks out once more, warning him, just as it had warned him earlier about talking too freely to Quando.* Whoa! Careful! *it says.* Take no notice! It's nothing. It's nothing! It's nothing! *Three times, like a spell. But the other voice is strong. It rises in pitch and intensity.* Up! Up! Up! Yes! *it insists.*

And suddenly he is terrified and begins to scream: "I don't want it. I don't want it. I don't want to be twisted and changed." Fear is making him sick . . . he is actually going to be sick, rendingly sick. He is going to be torn in two.

WAKING

Roland woke! He woke, straining and retching, soaked with perspiration though the night around him was cool. More than cool: chilly! For a second or two all he could do was struggle with his convulsing stomach muscles. "Stop it!" he exclaimed, commanding his stomach to behave, just as if it were a disobedient dog. "Be still! Down! Down!" Little by little he relaxed against his crushed, damp pillow, set free from the curious triple life of his dream, back in real time once more.

That dream! Yet again! Exactly as it had been every other time he had dreamed it. That first dreaming must have engraved itself on him in some indelible way. Always supposing the first dream had really *been* a dream . . .

Careful, said the inner voice (familiar by now), intruding as it always did at this point, warning him off—not that he needed to be warned. *Take care.*

So Roland was careful. He made himself think vague thoughts of school instead. And slowly the repetitive sighing eased and retreated; honest silence repossessed him, filling his head once more. Roland was able to lie in the dark and think things over.

Of course, other people also had dreams that repeated themselves, but this one seemed even harder to understand now that he was seventeen than it had when he first dreamed it at three or four. Because who could imagine hanging in outer space and doing nothing except *being* there? Anyone set free from gravity would want to play some sort of somersaulting game, would want to kick out and dance among the suns, shouting, "Look at me!" And what was the endless word that had begun to sigh at him . . . that still sighed at him from time to time? It took concentration to hold that word at bay. And why did the sheer nonsense of this dream terrify him in the way that it invariably did? Why was it the harmless ending of the dream and not the darkness inside the coffin that frightened him so much? And why did he always wake out of it sweating and heaving? It was to do with the possibility of becoming something his father might not recognize. So why, when he was both frightened by it and impatient with the nonsense of it, did the dream also seem more important than anything going on in his outside life? And why, in spite of his fear, did he sometimes long to hang like a sun among other suns, set in a place into which he fitted perfectly? Maybe it was because he did not quite fit into any other place. "Fabuloso!" Roland exclaimed softly in the darkness, copying his father's voice. "Trickery," he added, uncertain if he was the trickster or the man who was being tricked. This trickery (if it was trickery) not only worked inside Roland's overcrowded, argumentative head—it seemed to work remarkably well for him in the outside world as well.

Three Pens, a Pie, and a Notebook

Mr. Hudson set a cardboard box on his desk, blinking at Roland in a judicial way as he did so. For some reason this single glance entirely changed Roland's mood. He knew at once that he was not going to be praised, something he had been anticipating. Whatever it was that had caused Mr. Hudson to hold him back from midday break was being heralded by an expression of disapproval—even, Roland realized incredulously, of contempt.

Flicking the box open, Mr. Hudson thrust his left hand into it with the confidence of a conjurer who *knew* he was going to whisk a rabbit from an empty hat. He drew out not a rabbit, but a plastic packet containing three fine-tipped pens—red, green, and blue—which he set down in front of Roland with grim deliberation. Plunging his hand into the box for a second and then a third time, he brought out something in a greasy paper bag and finally a thick notebook with a red cover.

Roland's reaction to these successive revelations must have satisfied a teacher trying to establish a small melodrama. His mouth fell open like an astonished mouth in some overacted TV sitcom. He was more taken aback than if Mr. Hudson really *had* produced a rabbit, and certainly far more alarmed. After shooting a startled glance at his English teacher, he looked back at the objects placed before him. A great blush swept through him, starting under his hair and then, driven by powerful shame, burning down through his cheeks, chest, and stomach. Of all the people in his class—in the school, even—Roland was famous for smart answers, but he had no answer to the silent accusation that those pens, the greasy bag, and that notebook were making as they lay before him.

"Well?" said Mr. Hudson at last. Roland gave a shrug so small it was nothing more than a convulsive twitch. He did not even try to look in the paper bag. He already knew what it must contain. Mr. Hudson was confronting him with the exact duplicates of the articles he had stolen only a week ago.

"It's not as if you couldn't afford to *buy* them," said Mr.

Hudson. "Shoplifting is a contemptible crime, don't you think?"

Roland remained silent. There was no excuse for it; there was not any true explanation—not one that made any sense, even to him. Here he was, seventeen years old, licensed to drive, a moderately well-to-do student, a prefect, with the prospect of scholarship exams coming up at the end of the year. Not only that, he was going out with Chris Glennie, who was possibly the brightest, and certainly the most beautiful, girl in the school. How could he have risked screwing things up by shoplifting three pens, a pie, and a notebook? All the same, that was what he *had* done. The pie was gone, eaten almost immediately, but in the drawer of his desk at home three pens in a plastic envelope, along with a red-covered notebook, exact twins to the objects Mr. Hudson had just set down in front of him, were lying, totally unused.

It had been one of those days—a day like today, for that matter—when he had been allowed to drive his mother's car to school, with the proviso that he bring home a few family groceries. He had parked, crossed the road opposite the café painted blue and silver, and turning right into the arched mall, walked along it into the ultimate temple of the supermarket. He could clearly remember the moment when the impulse overtook him, could even remember the people to the left and right of him, all busy acting on impulses of their own. A mother with a baby in a stroller went sliding past him. A couple of young women were fidgeting by the rack of greeting cards, showing the cards to each other and laughing as they did so. Just beyond them a man in a long black coat held out a length of wrapping paper and stared down at it, apparently trying to work out if it was wide enough for his needs. The notebook slipped into Roland's back pocket just as easily as the package of pens, less than a minute later, slid inside his open collar to nestle over his heart, the bulge well hidden by the Crichton Academy blazer. Earlier he had chosen a pie from a small oven set at eye level on the wall in the fast-food section and had placed it carefully in the shopping cart among the groceries his mother needed. Moving into the frozen-food section he had leaned across the handle of the shopping cart and, easing the pie out of its paper bag, had begun to eat it, almost absent-mindedly. No one had seemed to notice, not even the young woman who had suddenly rounded the low open-refrigerated section, advancing on him briskly in her blue supermarket smock. He remembered looking at her defiantly, expecting some sort of accusation. But she must have been concentrating on some internal supermarket errand, for she had hurried on without so much as glancing at him.

And now it appeared that Mr. Hudson must have been somewhere close at hand—must have been spying on him down some oblique supermarket vista and must have been watching him closely enough to know the colors of the stolen pens and just which notebook he had chosen. And then he had obviously chosen for himself the exact objects he had seen Roland stealing, presumably to add drama to this confrontation. Cheap *drama,* thought Roland, staring at his teacher with tattered defiance.

"Why did you *do* it?" asked Mr. Hudson again. ("Why did *you*?" Roland wanted to retort, surveying the objects on the desk in front of him.)

"Dunno!" he said. To his embarrassment, his voice came

out as a guilty mumble. It had been a long time since he said anything in any teacher's presence that sounded so furtive and defeated. These days, if he was reprimanded (which occasionally still happened), he mostly succeeded in finding a reply that was literary or witty enough to win a reluctant grin. Mind you, it was a tricky thing to bring off. Clever answers could sometimes infuriate teachers who weren't in the mood for them. It was important to get the balance right. Roland had always believed, however, that he had Mr. Hudson well and truly sussed. For one thing, Mr. Hudson was a terrific reader and responded warmly to other readers, and Roland vaguely imagined that at the end of the year, when school was finally over, they would shrug off their unnatural roles of teacher and pupil and would become friends of a sort, talking about books when they met and joking with each other in a worldly way.

"I can't just let it go," said Mr. Hudson. "I can't overlook it." He waited, but Roland had nothing useful to say.

"I've obviously thought it over for a day or two," said Mr. Hudson. "You do realize, don't you, that if I went to the principal, *he* wouldn't overlook it, no matter how sorry you said you were. He is a little, well, let's say *obsessed* with the Crichton Academy image out on the street—which happens to mean behavior in public places, such as supermarkets." Roland thought of the school principal, Mr. McDonald, who had never seemed to be impressed by Roland's wit. "I don't think he'd necessarily *expel* you, or anything like that," Mr. Hudson went on, giving Roland a faintly relenting smile as he spoke. Then he paused, looking at Roland in a measuring way before completing his sentence. "But I think he'd probably have you struck off as a prefect." Roland, who had been about to relax and even to smile a little himself, relieved at detecting the smallest degree of camaraderie, felt his face stiffening once more as he imagined the guessing and gossip that would blaze up around the school if he were toppled in any way. His friends probably wouldn't desert him (though some of them might find their tolerance blurred with scorn and secret triumph), but his mother—his mother would be as degraded as if she had been caught shoplifting herself. The thought of his mother's humiliation struck him like pain. As for Chris—sexy Chris, with the long legs and the small, sharp breasts (dulled and camouflaged during the week by the Crichton school uniform, but joyously outlined by her weekend clothes)—Chris was ruthless with losers. Shoplifting! She'd dump him. No question. And then, as these thoughts flicked wildly through his head, it suddenly came to Roland that Mr. Hudson was working his way toward not a punishment, but a proposition. He looked up from the pens, the pie, and the notebook and studied his teacher warily.

AN ALARMING PROPOSITION

"Help me to discharge my conscience," Mr. Hudson now suggested, right on cue. "Give me the illusion of having done something constructive about your stupidity, and I won't go to the top about it. What do you say?"

He was about to propose a deal. Roland was flooded with such relief that he began blushing for the second time in five minutes. Still, he knew he couldn't afford to feel at ease just yet.

"There's a girl in your class who's having some sort

of problem," said Mr. Hudson. "Don't ask me how I know about it. I just know. Let's leave it at that. But I don't know exactly what her problem *is.* I'd like you to, well . . ." He paused. "I'd like you to take a bit of interest in her. Cultivate her. Find out what's happening in her life and report back to me. Do you think you could bring that off?"

It was almost worse than being told he must confess to the principal—almost, but not quite.

"Who is it?" Roland asked in a resigned voice.

Mr. Hudson's sigh was nearly inaudible. Roland's apprehension suddenly deepened.

"Jess Ferret," said Mr. Hudson, and (as Roland's mouth fell open in silent protest) he added hastily, holding up his hands, palms outward, and shaking them at Roland as if he might need to ward him off, "I know she's not one of your crowd, but—"

"She's not part of anyone's crowd." Roland was dismayed enough to interrupt him. "Sir, the Weasel—Jess Ferret, that is—*likes* being on her own. She *says* she does. I can't push in on her. It wouldn't work. I just can't."

"Are you telling me that someone as self-confident as you can't talk your way into a conversation with poor old Jess?" asked Mr. Hudson derisively. "After all, you talk your way *out* of plenty of situations—well, maybe not shoplifting," he added rather meanly, "but I've heard you in action over and over again by now. *And* you've known Jess for years. It's not as if she's a total stranger."

"Sir, everyone knows that Jess likes to be left alone," said Roland, ashamed at the desperation in his voice. He was sounding utterly uncool.

"Something's *happened* to her over the last day or two," Mr.

Hudson persisted. "I want to know what it is. And as to her saying she likes to be alone, well, I don't suppose it occurs to you that that's what people sometimes say when they feel they're going to be left alone anyway. They pretend, even to themselves, that it's what they wanted all along. And just in case you're in any doubt—no, I'm certainly not asking you to make a . . ." He hesitated. "A *close* friend of her. All I'm asking is that you take a bit of interest in her and see if you can't get her to confide in you a little. I mean, look at it this way—you've got status in the school, and she'll probably be flattered, deep down. She just might confide in you. And then you can report back to me. Once I've got a clearer picture of what's going on, I'll take over."

It suddenly occurred to Roland that, even allowing for the fact that a caring teacher might scheme on behalf of some pupil who seemed at risk, there was something peculiar about this assignment. His eyes narrowing, he lifted his head and for the first time stared directly at Mr. Hudson, only to catch a flicker of something eager yet furtive coming and going behind that expression of official concern. Their glances locked. Then Mr. Hudson looked down rather quickly at the pens and notebook on his desk, drawing in a hissing half breath, which he managed to turn into casual emphasis but which was far from casual. When he looked up again, his expression was nothing if not bland and judicial once more. *What's going on?* Roland wanted to know. *What's really going on?* But at that moment he felt too unsure of himself to ask.

"Well, I'll try," he said, giving in. He had no real choice. "But she mightn't want to . . . I mean, what if she tells me to get lost?"

Mr. Hudson smiled a little. "Don't worry about what she *might* say." Roland could almost feel him relaxing, there on the other side of the pens, the pie, and the red notebook. "If she's stubborn—well, we'll talk about other possibilities. But for the present I suggest you get into conversation with her—you know, talk about books . . . films . . . cricket . . . whatever she's interested in. She does read a lot. Oh, and science! She's keen on science. Her father's some sort of scientist. Ask about him, if you like. Her mother works, and so does yours. You've got something in common. Tell her about your parents and see if you can't find out about hers. Parents are reasonably universal territory, aren't they? We've all got them. Is it a deal?"

But this was no deal. It was an order.

"Yes, sir. Okay! But—"

"'But me no buts!'" quoted Mr. Hudson, smiling now, not even trying to hide his pleasure that things were going the way he wanted them to go.

But . . ., echoed Roland's inner voice, that cautioning voice that had first spoken to him in his old nightmare. *But . . .*, it repeated, without having any more to say.

And a few minutes later Roland was walking down the school corridor, feeling a stranger to himself. Twenty minutes ago he had been in charge of his life. Now he was tottering on the edge of disgrace. *But . . .*, repeated that inner voice.

And this time something contrary and irrational leaped up inside him. It was as if he had been secretly hoping . . . well, certainly not for this, but for something dangerous and wild—something to override his everyday life, even though he had worked so steadily over the last seven years to set that responsible life firmly in place.

THE VIEW ACROSS THE SCHOOL YARD

Roland crossed the long yard between the school and the school library, wondering if he would find it possible to eat the lunch he had made for himself that morning. As he walked toward the library a sound that was not quite a sound assailed him. There it was again—that intricate *breathing*—bursting in on him, as it did from time to time, no matter how he tried to exclude it. *Up, up, up! Up and out! Out! Transform, transform!* It seemed, right then, like a command whispered with great privacy into his ear. *Transform!* it ordered him. *Ignore it,* his inner voice advised him, as it always did. *Keep clear.*

Mr. Hudson was right about one thing, at least. Roland had known Jess Ferret for a long time. They shared a birthday, and twelve years ago they had started school together. So Jess had been in his class for as long as he could remember, sitting, year after year, in desk after desk, more or less halfway down classroom after classroom, rarely putting her hand up or demanding attention in the way that he or Chris or Tom or Stephen did. Jess answered most of the questions she was asked in a serious, sluggish voice, and puttered along, doing well enough in most things. But she never quite made it to that top group with whom teachers exchanged sly jokes—the ones who read sophisticated books, firing quotations like arrows at one another, and dragging evidence of trendy reading into classroom discussion. Roland turned Jess over in his mind as he automatically looked for Chris, Tom, and the rest of his gang. There they were, dominating the seats outside, just below the windows of the school library, as they usually did during lunch hour.

"What did Hudson want?" Shelley Randall asked Roland as

he collapsed, with exaggerated ease, into a space at the end of one of the benches.

"Oh, he wanted to remind me how great I was," Roland replied, flicking his hand carelessly. "No big deal! Knew it already!" They sat under the library windows, partly because it was sunny there, even in winter, but also because the library was on a slight rise and gave them a dominant view across the school yard, past a few well-established trees to the western end of the football field. As Roland answered, gesturing grandly and almost spilling his sandwiches, he was peering between a broad scatter of fellow pupils to a particular seat under a particular, distant linden tree. Yes! There she was, as big and boring as ever. Jess Ferret. Mr. Hudson was right. It would be pathetically easy to get her attention. But not now. There was no natural way he could leave his friends and casually stroll over to talk to her without inviting derisive speculation and probably embarrassing Jess into total silence. Working out a few possible tactics, he stared across at her, while Chris and Tom slung off at him, telling him he was so far up himself that one day he'd come strolling out of his own mouth. *Jess Ferret,* thought Roland. Why did it have to be Jess Ferret of all people? Even the name Ferret was a school joke. ("*Question!* Which girl out there is Jess Ferret? *Answer!* You can weaselly tell, because she looks stoatally different.") She did quite well in mathematics, he recalled, but then, mathematicians were a nerdy lot. "Imagination beats calculation," he had once declared, feeling he'd summed it up pretty well. Yet now, looking over at that solitary figure under the linden tree, Roland found himself wondering how he could possibly have spent hours each day, for years and years, in the same space as another person and still know so little about her. He seemed to remember that she was an only child, but realized he wasn't quite sure about this. Mr. Hudson had said that her father was a scientist, but that didn't explain much—he could be a geologist or a physicist, or could be, as far as Roland knew, involved in putting sheep genes into cows so that they would provide wool as well as milk. And Mr. Hudson had talked about her mother, so apparently she had one of each (unlike *some* people, he reminded himself). He thought he might recognize her mother if he saw her, but not her father. And what sort of car did they drive? Or, come to that, did they drive at all? He did not even know where Jess lived—somewhere in the city, of course, but whereabouts exactly? He had the impression that she always walked everywhere, so presumably her home was not far from the school.

"Whoo-hoo! Wake up," called Chris, waving her hand in front of his face. "Stop dreaming about me! Here! This way! I'm over here, being sexy and fascinating."

"He's wallowing in Hudson's praise," said Tom, and Roland saw, rather to his surprise, that Tom really did believe that Mr. Hudson had kept him back to make flattering comments on his work. After all, it was what he had half expected himself. But Chris knew better.

"La, la, la!" she sang, looking over at Tom with her usual good-natured mockery. "He's having you on, Tommy. Old Hudson gave him a rocket about something. He's been taken down. I can tell."

If he confessed to some fault, he'd get them off his back. They'd have a good laugh at his humiliation and then forget it. Roland tried a foolish grin, though foolish grins were not part of his usual repertoire.

WESTFIELD PUBLIC LIBRARY
333 West Hoover Street
Westfield, IN 46074

"I blew it over that Kiwi film piece," he said, inventing quickly. "I just put down the first shit that came into my head, and Hudson decided to have a crack at me. You know! 'You're not in my class to coast along! Blah! Blah! Blah!' Like that!"

"It's what he's paid to say," said Tom tolerantly. "Probably a way of reminding himself he's still alive."

"And anyhow, Roley *enjoys* coasting along," Chris put in.

"Roley by name, Roley by nature," said Roland, shifting his gaze from Jess Ferret to Chris. Only yesterday afternoon, sitting in her bedroom, she had half sighed, half sobbed into his shoulder, "I do want to . . . I do. . . ." But having said this, she had added that her mother would be home soon and had pulled away from him. Now she was deliberately reminding him, Roland supposed, that she still belonged to herself. Their eyes met. She gave him her crooked smile, which always reminded him of someone beckoning, then turned toward Stephen and Shelley once more.

"We're off to the West Coast this weekend," she said. "The weather forecast's great. I'm going to smother myself in cream, lie naked in the sun, and read."

"You'll be bitten all over by sand flies," said Tom, while Roland, certain she was deliberately making this comment so that his head would be filled with the image of her nakedness, stared briefly at her neck and her fair hair, caught back in a short, thick braid.

"Dream on!" he said, looking away once more. "Even if it's fine, it'll be miles too cold to swim, let alone sunbathe."

Out under the linden tree, Jess was closing her book. Roland, gobbling the last of his lunch, determined not to waste it after he had gone to the trouble of making it, suddenly wanted to know what she was reading. Jess stretched her arm out, then hooked it back—to consult a watch, he supposed. It was a real watch-consulting gesture; though, of course, he couldn't be sure, not from where he was sitting. As she did this the bell rang. It was almost as if she had accurately anticipated the first stroke.

"Your lot are picking you up straight after school, aren't they?" he asked Chris as they began to walk, side by side, toward the door nearest their classroom.

"'Fraid so!" she said, assuming he was a little melancholy at the prospect of a weekend without her. "Never mind! It'll just whisk away—Saturday! Sunday! La, la, la." She incessantly used fragments of song to emphasize or punctuate her dialogue, or to suggest that she couldn't be bothered spelling things out to anyone too stupid to anticipate what she meant.

Roland nodded vaguely.

"Go on!" Chris said, nudging him. "Try to sound a bit sorry that you're not coming with us."

"Well, actually, I've lined up a date with someone who's crazy about me," he replied. He and Chris often pretended to each other that they had a string of secret admirers, but on this occasion his voice sounded flat and automatic in his own ears, rather as if he were giving out a recorded message.

"That's right," said Chris approvingly. "Make the best of it! Brave you!" She spoke without the slightest fear that anyone could ever win his attention away from her. "So will I! La, la, la!" she sang, smiling at him as if she knew all his secrets. And indeed she did know quite a few of them.

UNEXPECTED DIFFICULTIES

After school Chris drove off with her parents, who were waiting for her at the main back gate of the school in their four-wheel-drive. She slung her pack onto the backseat, then scrambled in, flashing her long, elegant legs as she pulled herself up onto the high step. Grasping the edge of the door, she twisted around to wave, then, a moment later, he saw her beaming and waving again, framed in the rear window as they drove away. Roland shot one arm into the air, grinning as he did so. Only he knew that he was merely copying his usual self. The framed image of Chris diminished and disappeared, waving to the last.

"Oh, man! She's a real cockteaser," Stephen said, and waited for some sort of denial or perhaps a knowing grin—anything that might give him a clue as to how far Chris and Roland had gone with each other. It was easy for Roland to fall silent, smiling enigmatically and giving nothing away. He already had Jess Ferret in his sights. There she was, wandering toward the small gate at the back of the school, talking to two other girls as she went.

"Okay, mate! See you, then," Stephen was saying, turning toward the bike shed, and setting Roland free to jog after the three girls, ready to perfect an accidental approach. Halfway across the intervening space Mr. Hudson came striding toward him, and Roland wondered if he might be about to get some sort of extra instruction, but Mr. Hudson walked on in the general direction of the staff parking lot, looking past Roland and waving to someone as he went. Glancing back over his shoulder, Roland saw two women (probably mothers), a man in a black coat, and his fellow prefect Tom over by the bike shed doing a prefect's check on those Crichton pupils who were claiming their bikes and who were all supposed to be wearing approved cycling helmets. Nobody, as far as he could see, was waving back to Mr. Hudson. Roland jogged on.

"'Childe Roland to the dark tower came,'" he muttered, quoting a line he occasionally called on in a joking way—the first line of a ballad by some nineteenth-century poet. He knew that the word *childe* meant "a young man of noble birth," but almost nobody else knew this, so he used it as a secret joke. Over by the gate the three girls were moving away from one another, two going right (one waving, one walking backward for a few steps) while Jess turned through the gate and set off quickly along the street. Roland sped up. He overtook her and said, "Oh! Hi!" in a voice so mildly surprised and casual that it pleased him. But she did not reply, and glancing sideways, he saw her mop of badly cut, slightly frizzy black curls was tilted away from him. "Hi!" he repeated rather more insistently, and this time his voice must have registered, for she slowly turned her familiar, round, blank face toward him. She wore the expression of someone waking, a little unwillingly, from a dream—a dream that must have taken her over during the few minutes she had been walking on her own.

"Hi!" said Roland for the third time. "Yes! Right! It's you I'm talking to. Penny for them!"

"What?" she replied.

"Your thoughts," he said. "You must have been thinking of *something.*"

"Whatever I was thinking of was worth a hell of a lot more

than a penny," Jess replied, taking him by surprise. He had not expected such sharp words to come from such a vacant face. Suddenly, though, Jess Ferret was far from vacant. Suddenly she was all there—guarded, almost aggressive.

"Yeah?" Roland asked. "Okay! So how much do you reckon they're worth? Give me an estimate."

"Miles more than you could ever afford," she replied, and though she still sounded irritated, she smiled sideways at him in her particular Weaselly-Ferret way. Back in the days when she had to wear braces on her teeth, Jess had taken to smiling with her lips closed, which was how she smiled now—a smile directed outward into the world, but inward, too, back into some secret cave of thought where she stored a bit of unexpected mockery and sarcasm. Roland found he was disconcerted because she did not seem to be sufficiently impressed to have him walking beside her. He was instantly annoyed with her, but annoyed with himself, too. He had caught himself being bigheaded again.

"Go on! Try me!" he said. But to his surprise, Jess, without warning, stopped dead and turned to face him.

"Okay!" she exclaimed. "What do you want?"

Roland came to a standstill too.

"Nothing!" he said a little incredulously. "I was just—you know—saying something slightly friendly as I walked by. What's the big deal?"

"But you're not walking by. You're *aiming* yourself at me," she declared.

"Don't you just wish!" exclaimed Roland. "Hey! I promise it wasn't any major move."

"No, but it's *some* sort of a move," she said, surprising him with her certainty. "Do you want help with your math homework? Or is it a dare? Or what?"

She was right, of course. It was some sort of move. All the same, Roland felt as indignant as a man who is falsely accused of being a stalker.

"Oh, wow!" he said. "I'll know better than to try out any friendly conversation on *you* again." And he mimed zipping his lips together.

"Fair enough!" she said, and then surprised him yet again by turning the words almost back to front. "Air and fluff!" she added, grinning to herself as she walked on without once looking behind her.

The trouble was Roland couldn't allow her to walk away. He had to set up some sort of useful dialogue so that he could satisfy bloody old self-righteous Hudson. And suddenly there was a little more to it than that. Why should a reasonably plain, ordinary girl—one with bushy black hair, a slightly greasy fringe, and a pimple forming just above her left temple—respond in such a careless fashion when one of the top guys in the school spoke to her? Still standing, Roland called after her.

"No! Hang on a moment!"

Jess turned but kept on walking . . . walking backward with surprising confidence.

"The thing is . . . ," said Roland, rapidly improvising around an earlier thought and advancing cautiously as he spoke, "I was thinking at lunchtime how mad it was that there were people in our room that I've known for years and years—I mean people like Dick Peebles and Cathy Morpeth and you—and yet we've never really *said* anything to one another. I mean, you and me—we *have* talked about the weather two or three times, but that's not much, is it, over twelve years or so. . . ." He broke off and shrugged, falling silent and waiting to see what she might make of this declaration.

Jess's expression changed. Now it was her turn to come to a stop, right in the middle of the sidewalk. But then, without turning, she stepped to one side so that an elderly woman could walk past her unobstructed. There was something a little eerie about the accuracy with which she had moved out of the way at exactly the right moment.

"So you reckon I ought to be bowled over by you bending down out of the clouds and talking to me?" she asked.

"Yes," he almost said, which would have been true. "No!" he exclaimed, anxious to wipe away her perfectly justifiable suspicion. "I just thought we'd talk a little as we walked along—that's all. No big deal!" He was walking toward her, taking small, smooth, unthreatening steps, and at least she was not retreating.

"Talk? What would *we* talk about?" she asked.

"Anything. . . . Pets! Parents!" He shrugged, then remembered something useful. "Books! You can read, can't you? I've seen you at it. What are you reading?"

For some reason this question, simple enough when asked between one reader and another, seemed to disconcert her.

"That's my business," she said. "Look, Fairfield! I *like* being on my own, and having to talk to anyone ruins it all. You're *stalking* me, but your talk spoils—and your stalk toils!"

Roland had to disentangle this.

"What does it spoil?" he asked, almost wanting to know.

"*It!*" she answered, smiling, once again, her outward-inward smile. "Don't you know what *it* means?"

Roland knew she was quoting something though couldn't

quite remember what, which was annoying for someone who himself was good at quoting. But at least they were talking once more, and he was once more looking into her eyes, eyes of a strong blue color with—now that he came to look at them closely—long, sweeping black lashes and wide black pupils.

And then a peculiar thing happened. The irises and pupils of Jess Ferret's eyes changed. Irises and pupils seemed to collapse into each other—to contract into long, intense slits of darkness. But before he could be sure of what he was seeing in them, they separated once more into perfectly normal irises and pupils.

Roland opened his mouth, fully expecting words to spring obediently out of it, but for once the tip of his tongue (that springboard from which they usually leaped so eagerly) was empty. He and Jess stared at each other for a full second longer. Then she laughed and turned, heading toward the main road. She walked so firmly that her footsteps seemed to echo, and Roland had a momentary illusion that there was something invisible following at her heels.

There was no point, he thought, in pursuing her and trying to force any more conversation out of someone so unwilling to talk, and yet he couldn't give up. He just had to feel he'd gained some territory. "'Stalk toils,'" he quoted to himself, and turning, he began to jog once more, patting his pocket to make sure the keys of his mother's car were still safely in place. It was one thing for Chris Glennie to drive off, waving lightheartedly out of the back window. It was quite a different thing for Weaselly-Ferret to turn her back on him and stump away without casting a single glance over her shoulder. "'Air and fluff,' eh?" he muttered as he ran. "We'll see!"

Careful, advised his inner voice, probably already aware that, this time at least, he was going to ignore it.

Roland reached the car, unlocked it, and scrambled into the driver's seat, tossing his pack behind him. Glancing quickly into the rearview mirror, he swung into the road. But when he looked in front of him once more, Jess had vanished. His impression was that she must have turned to the right. After all, she had been on the right-hand sidewalk when he had last seen her. Gunning the engine like a driver in a television road chase, he reached the end of the street and swung dramatically into the busy main road only to find that his life as a tracker had become much more complicated. He was now part of a stream of traffic. Scanning the sidewalks for any sign of Jess Ferret wasn't easy.

A COMPLICATED PURSUIT

Roland was now driving through a familiar shopping center with cars moving slowly in front of him and closing in from behind. On his left he saw a favorite café and, directly beside it, the flamboyant arched opening to a mall crowded with shoppers. The entrance, illuminated even in daylight, often reminded Roland of the entrance to a church, somehow suggesting that shopping in the supermarket at the end of the mall would be a mystical experience.

A cluster of five Crichton girls stood peering in the windows of a trendy dress shop, talking and passing a bag around. Strictly speaking, it was Roland's job as a prefect to remind them that they were not supposed to eat in the street while wearing the school uniform, but right then it was impossible to be an efficient stalker and a prefect, as well as a responsible driver. It came as a relief when the traffic lights turned red and he was able to come to a legitimate standstill. As people streamed across the road in front of him he hastily scanned the sidewalks from right to left, knowing as he did so that Jess could be looking at him from any of the shops and laughing at him. Tilting the rearview mirror, he tried to check the five girls behind him in more detail. But then the light changed and he was obliged to shoot off again, jolting in a way that did not match his image of himself as a competent and cool driver.

Then he saw her. Once he had her in his sights, he wondered how he could ever have imagined that any one of the girls peering into the dress shop could possibly have been Jess Ferret. She suddenly seemed unique. Anxious to keep her under surveillance, he tried to slow down, but the car behind him tooted sharply, forcing him to accelerate, to drive briefly alongside his quarry, then on past her. Desperate to keep her in view, he pulled in illegally at a bus stop. Two boys with skateboards were also making use of this space, bumping over the edge of the gutter, then bouncing back onto the pavement once more. One of them gave Roland the finger as he moved in on their territory, but Roland was too preoccupied to take any notice. He was simultaneously tilting the rearview mirror and shrinking down in his seat as Jess came striding toward him. Then she walked past, looking neither right nor left, and moved ahead of him once more. A useful space appeared in the traffic flow. Roland hastily pulled out into it, anxious to take advantage of any good luck the capricious city might be offering him. But as he took possession of the lucky space, grinning with relief, Jess disappeared. He could hardly believe it. One moment she had been there, caught in the mirror. Then she was gone. It was as if she had never existed.

As he struggled with surprise Roland saw, some distance ahead of him, a silver car pulling out and leaving an empty parking space. He parked in it, and now he saw a sign he did not remember noticing before, though he had been up and down this road so many times. Perhaps it was there only if you knew where to look for it. An enameled arrow, made almost invisible by layers of dirt and dust, pointed into a narrow slot between two buildings, and below the arrow were the words RIVERLAW RESERVE ACCESS. Up until now he had always walked past the paved alley the arrow was indicating, vaguely thinking it must be a private entrance of some kind. Now he peered hesitantly between largely featureless concrete walls. Garbage bags jostled one another around a few closed doors, apart from which the lane was quite empty. All the same, Jess Ferret must have turned in here. There was no other possibility. Snaking between the garbage bags, Roland set off in pursuit.

He came out into a space that took him by surprise. Directly in front of him was a wide road, and beyond the road ran a stream, its neat green banks planted with intermittent willows. The road on this side of the stream was obviously used for the most part by trucks and vans coming and going between the loading bays that extended from the backs of various shops. But looking across to the other side of the stream, Roland saw a parallel road and a row of houses—old houses, but well cared for, their hedges and gardens neat and tidy, their walls cleanly painted. At that particular moment there seemed to be nothing moving. It was like stepping onto a deserted stage set. "Riverlaw," he said to himself, and began to remember.

Here it was, a small suburb tucked away behind the mall. Years ago the residents had passionately resisted the rezoning that had allowed the supermarket development. There had been petitions and letters to the paper declaring that the riverbank should be sacrosanct. Property values had dropped. Many people had moved away. For no matter how pleasantly maintained the riverbanks were, no matter how beautiful the willows might be in early spring, the pleasure of walking under them must have been reduced by the intrusive proximity of shop yards, parked vans, cartons, and almost certainly, a lot of anonymous refuse.

Roland looked around wildly. There! There! Movement! A single moving figure—a Crichton school uniform crossing a narrow footbridge that arched over the stream a little to his right. "Yes!" he hissed triumphantly. "Jess Ferret!" She hadn't managed to shed *him.* He was on her trail.

This time he had her in clear sight. He did not have to worry about any cars ahead of him or those closing in impatiently from behind. There were no doorways or crowds in which she might lose herself. If she had turned, she might have seen him and would no doubt have recognized him just as easily as he was able to recognize her. But she did not turn. She simply crossed the bridge, the footpath that ran along the opposite bank, and finally the road in front of her. Moving a little unwillingly, Roland slid out from the protection of the shop walls, preparing to track her at a discreet distance.

But Jess had arrived at what must be her house. She was walking past a blue mailbox up a long drive between two neat hedges toward a tall, two-storied building set back behind other houses but peering enigmatically out over them. Heading toward the footbridge himself, Roland watched her as she made for a green front door, then hesitated in front of it, fumbling in her bag. *She's looking for her keys,* he thought. *That means there's no one at home yet.* As he speculated Jess found her key, unlocked the door, and stepped through. The door seemed to spring shut behind her as if it were every bit as anxious as she seemed to be to keep the outside world at bay. She was gone.

Roland suddenly began to laugh silently to himself, shaking his head as he did so. *Fabuloso!* said his inner voice sarcastically, making fun not only of the world, but of Roland himself. What a day! *Not now,* his inner voice instructed him. *Think about all that later.* So! Dreary old Jess Ferret had imagined she could just shrug him off. Well, he had been too clever for her, hadn't he? He now knew where she lived—there, directly across the river.

In spite of the frustrations of the hunt, Roland realized he had enjoyed himself and, unexpectedly, was still enjoying himself, alone in this overlooked piece of the city. He knew that the stream must be Carlings Brook, a tributary of the main river. Under the willows below these gates, close to the river's edge, was a picnic table that seemed somehow surreal. A bulletin board caught his eye. There were to be stalls and raffles there next Wednesday afternoon. There was to be a magician. Riverlaw Kindergarten was hoping to raise money for its equipment fund.

Roland crossed the strip of green to look down into the water. For all its sleek, soft flow it was edged not only with living watercress, but with sodden cartons, cigarette butts, anonymous strips of plastic, and Coke cans. *Flow, flow, flow,* something said, breathing into him as if it were trying to dissolve into his blood and negotiate his pumping heart. That delicate chatter began once more. *Unfolding, unfolding, transform, transform, transform!*

Back away, his inner voice warned him. *Careful! Back away!*

So Roland backed away by thinking of his car waiting out on the main road beside a hungry parking meter. *Home,* he thought. *I'll go home now.* As he walked up the lane once more he puzzled not over the breathy inner chattering (which he always preferred to ignore), but over his inexplicable moment of exhilaration. Realizing he was grinning with pleasure, he reined in his wide smile but then shrugged and let it spread again. Why not grin? Why not enjoy what was happening whenever he could? An adventure! *I'll work it out later,* he thought. Heading for the car, he saw, to his horror, that a parking warden was standing beside it, writing out a ticket.

Roland marched forward as the warden moved on, and snatched the ticket from behind the windshield wiper, grimacing as he did so. Frowning down at the ticket, he felt himself changing back from being Roland the mysterious huntsman into Roland the man of the family who must soon make some sort of confession to his mother. And this confession would probably have to be made in front of his two younger brothers—nine-year-old Danny and Martin, who was seven, both of whom watched him perpetually, waiting for him to make the sort of mistakes that would bring him down to their own level.

REMEMBERING MIDNIGHT TEARS

For the first few months after his father disappeared, Roland would wake in the night to hear his mother crying in the darkness of her room, across the hall from his. She would be feeding the new baby and weeping wearily, almost as if she were lamenting in her sleep. The sound of that sadness, faint though it was, had pushed its way out relentlessly from under her door and in under his.

Roland had been ten years old when Martin was born, and his father had left them. When he thought back, it somehow seemed to Roland that as his mother had staggered out the front door, desperately counting money for the taxi fare (and pausing every so often to concentrate on the sort of breathing that would urge her unborn baby out into the world), his father had been racing through the *back* door, also eager to catch a taxi but not the same one. His father's taxi would whisk him to the airport so that he could fly up and away, leaving them all behind him. It was a long time ago now, years ago, but though he hoped his mother's tears were over and done with, he was never quite sure. Certainly the sound of her sadness had spread itself backward and forward through time, and whenever he was able to tell her of some new school achievement, he was aware of a hidden pleasure in the idea that he might be balancing things out for her. Sometimes he felt with dismay that he, and he alone, stood between his mother and the lurking sadness that was still there, waiting to move in on her once more.

"You do look like your father," she would say in a shy voice, for she knew that Roland did not want to look like anyone but himself. "He was very good-looking," she would add defensively. Good-looking or not, Roland did not want to resemble in any way the man who had taken half the family money out of the bank and who had shot off—first to Australia, then to Canada—never to be seen again. Yet though she might have wept at night, during the day Roland's mother ("the indomitable Mrs. Fairfield," he had once heard the principal of his school call her) had been staunch. She had found an office job, taken a night course in computer skills, and worked hard and long. Life had occasionally buckled and sometimes even snapped during the first two years, but Mrs. Fairfield had twisted everything back into some sort of shape . . . had mended or half mended the breaks, so that things worked well enough to get from one day to the next. Slowly she had won power over her altered world and had been able to afford first a better nursery for the baby, Martin, and then, when the time came for Roland to go to prep school, fees for a school that was officially admired and (unofficially) resented for the good opinion it had of itself.

"I know it's a struggle to send me to Crichton," Roland had once said tentatively. "I could just as easily go to Huntsbury High, you know."

"Oh, no!" his mother had cried, just as he had secretly hoped she would. "I'm sure Huntsbury is a good school, but Crichton has got something extra. They do really well when it comes to public exams and scholarships and so on. And style! It's got style! Everyone says so. And, oh boy, we need all the style we can get in this life."

Looking into an Invented Darkness

When Roland opened the door that evening, the sound of his brothers' perpetual arguments burst in on him. Hearing this familiar sound, he grimaced a little. His mother was sitting by the heater and reading a magazine—a rare, restful luxury for her. But then, Friday night was always an easy fast-food night for the Fairfields. A rising politician was holding forth on the television screen, tilting his eyebrows and smiling confidently as he spoke, but the sound was turned down so that Mrs. Fairfield's reading would not be interrupted. Glancing at the screen, Roland immediately recognized the speaker.

"That's old Hudson's brother," he remarked, his interest rather more sour than it would have been this time yesterday. "They reckon he's a future prime minister."

The future prime minister mouthed and gesticulated, but Roland's mother was not interested. Nevertheless, her face had brightened. As she stood up she gave him that familiar beaming smile he knew so well.

"So there you are at last," she cried. "Is the car all right? Did you remember to lock it?"

"Yes, of course," said Roland impatiently, tilting his left shoulder down so that his pack thumped onto the floor, while he dangled the car keys from his extended right hand. Amused by his irritation, his mother moved quickly on to the next question.

"So, what do you reckon? Pizza or Chinese?"

"Chinese," said Roland.

"Oh, well, that's that," said Mrs. Fairfield. "Now, give me a kiss!"

But Roland was determined to get his confession over and done with. "Mum, you mightn't want a kiss," he said. "Listen! I got a ticket. Sorry!" Danny and Martin, playing some game at the table, both looked up sharply. Their argument had concluded as he came into the room, allowing them to move into an unspoken alliance against him.

"Oh, damn!" his mother cried. "How on earth did you do that?"

"You must have really tried hard to get one," said Danny. Roland now saw that he and Martin were taking turns playing a pocket-size electronic game called *Viper*—a game that actually belonged to Roland himself. They must have stolen it from his room.

"*Really* hard!" chimed in Martin, Danny's obedient echo. They enjoyed trying to cut him down to their own size. The *Viper* game played its maddening electronic tune three times in quick succession. "My turn! My turn!" yelled Martin.

"It was out by the mall," explained Roland, speaking to his mother across the argument his brothers were now resuming. "I parked there for about fifteen minutes and—"

"But there's a great big supermarket parking lot across the road from the mall," cried his mother.

"Mum, I'm really sorry," Roland said again, guilty but impatient at having to apologize twice. "I thought I'd only be a minute—well, I *was* only a minute—a few minutes, anyway. . . ." His voice trailed away. "I'll pay," he offered rather stiffly. "I've still got that birthday money Grandpa sent me and—"

"Don't even think of it," his mother said impatiently. "You're not to spend Grandpa's present on a parking fine. Mind you, it's a pity, but . . ." Here she sighed with exaggerated force. "Anyway, just be more careful, that's all."

"You always say that to *him*," Danny shouted, then turned quickly as *Viper* peeped and sang again, this time between Martin's fingers.

"I don't *mind* paying," said Roland, ashamed at feeling a surge of relief. But of course he had known when he made the offer that there was a good chance his mother would turn it down. His brothers knew it too.

"He was just bullshitting," growled Danny. "He didn't mean it."

"Danny, I hate that language," said their mother. "It's real Huntsbury talk!" She was referring to Huntsbury High School, the main rival of Crichton Academy. "Just for that, you can be the one to go and collect the takeout—well, once we work out what we want. Where's that menu they gave us last time?" She looked over at Roland. "Grandpa would want you to spend that money on something you really enjoyed," she said.

"Roley enjoys Chinese food," suggested Martin. "He could buy us dinner with his birthday money."

"Right on!" shouted Danny. Once again the game took advantage of his distraction. "Oh, blast!"

"Serves you right for getting too smart," said Roland. And then there was a confused few minutes during which all three of them shouted at one another while their mother looked for the menu, finally locating it in a kitchen drawer. All four of them tried to work out just what meals they would be wanting, and a tremor of argument about what television they might watch while they ate their takeout came and went during this discussion. It all took time, but at last everything was decided, and, at last, Roland was able to think about making for the sanctuary of his room.

"And how's Chris?" his mother suddenly asked playfully. It was almost as if she were flirting with him herself.

"What about her?" asked Roland, turning a little defensively. At the mention of Chris's name both Danny and Martin looked up from the game of *Viper* and began a rude howling. Danny made terrible sucking sounds.

"Chris! Chris! Chris! How about a kiss?" he shouted. "Oh, what luck! We can have a—"

"Shut up!" yelled Mrs. Fairfield, cutting in just in time. "Stop it, you kids. I hate it when you speak like that. Just ignore them, Roland."

"I am! I do!" said Roland. "They can be as immature as they like. I don't care. Anyhow, Chris is away for the weekend . . . on the coast with her family. *And,* by the way, that's *my* game of *Viper.*" His brothers howled again, but this time with dismay, as Roland, stretching nimbly over Martin's shoulder, snatched the game away from them and pushed it into the pocket of his blazer. Then, hoisting his backpack once more, he made for his bedroom . . . his sanctuary.

But tonight when the bedroom door closed behind him, the events of the day came crashing over him like an avalanche. His backpack thumped on the floor and he tumbled forward onto his bed, boots on the quilt, face burying itself deep in his pillow. The family cat, Scruff, who had complacently folded himself beside the pillow, shot away, ears back, looking highly aggrieved. Finding the door firmly shut, he had no choice but to sit down and treat himself to a good, hard washing, while Roland lay on his bed, gazing into self-imposed darkness and feeling the weight of his remarkable afternoon bearing down on him. At first it seemed like a single weight between his shoulders, but then it divided, becoming not one burden but several. There was the central one, of course—his confrontation with Mr. Hudson. Then there was his failed attempt to command Jess Ferret's grateful attention, followed by the complicated excitement of tracking her home. And mixed in with all this was something else—something uneasy and shapeless, something he could not name. *I'm altering,* he thought.

Hey! his inner voice commanded him. *Forget all that! Pull yourself together, mate. You are what you are what you are! Don't try to be different!*

"I'm not trying to be different . . . ," he mumbled into his pillow, then broke off. "Oh, forget it!" he told himself impatiently.

Really, he thought, *I should tell old Hudson to get stuffed. I should tell him to go ahead and let McDonald know everything.* ("Old McDonald had a school," he and his friends had sung years ago. "Ee-i-ee-i-o! And every teacher was a fool! Ee-i-ee-i-o!") He had already argued his way through all this earlier in the afternoon, but he couldn't help going through it again and again and again. Okay, so if he *did* confess to the principal, it would mean having to surrender his prefect's badge, but then, at least, the whole business would be behind him—over and done with, and there would be none of this sneaking around trying to strike up conversations with Jess Ferret and being rejected with something close to scorn. And after a week or two some other school scandal would push his doings into the background. Most people would quickly forget his fall from grace.

But then the mocking image of Chris swam in his mind—really swam because, for some reason, he found himself imagining her stroking toward him, gliding through rippling green water, slender and naked, with her hair billowing out around her. And then, before he had a chance to enjoy this vision in any way, his mother became part of it too, dog-paddling alongside Chris in her own determined fashion, wearing last year's navy blue swimsuit. Roland groaned softly. Chris's probable scorn and his mother's inevitable grief were not to be borne. Why . . . why . . . why had he stolen anything in the first place? That was the rocky question. Why?

Turning his head wearily, as if it were a dead weight that had to be rolled along rather than lifted up, he stared at his desk, half imagining he might, if he really concentrated, be able to see where the pens and the red notebook were still hidden, a somehow sinister presence in the darkness of a closed drawer. And at that moment, probably because the closed drawer suddenly reminded him of a coffin, the ancient and irrelevant dream of the magician, Quando, slid into his mind. *Careful!* Impatiently Roland chased both the warning voice and the memory out of his head.

And, after all, he had half expected the voice. What he had not expected was that a strange, irritated exhilaration should suddenly be active in him, edging its way through the humiliations of the day, glinting like a random gold thread in the dark weave of the afternoon. He had first felt it leap into life as Stephen turned away from him in the school yard, as if from that moment on he was set free of family and friends—even free of Chris—to live a life that would be exclusively his own. Of course, having to talk to Jess had been a bit of a drag, though that moment when she had suddenly stopped looking so utterly vacant and had snapped back at him was something to think about. But how could he possibly have enjoyed tracking her—stalking her, really, though the word *stalking* had an ugly sound to it. *Stalk toils!* Roland groaned again. He did not want thoughts of Jess Ferret to feel enjoyable in any way. And he did not want to think too much about that odd, sharp glance that Mr. Hudson, his hitherto favorite teacher, had given him . . . a glance that suggested he was being *used* in some secret way and was not being told what was really going on.

Well, he had the whole weekend ahead of him. It wasn't as if Mr. Hudson had ordered him to come up with a written report on the Weasel by Monday, or anything. And then, as Roland sustained himself by contemplating a couple of free days, he caught himself remembering Jess's blue eyes looking at him under her long black lashes, and the way her irises and pupils had merged into intense slits—slits that had seemed like peepholes to another universe—before immediately opening out into ordinary eyes once more. Here, alone in his bedroom, he was able to puzzle about that moment. If he had had the chance to look into those slits, would he have seen the curve of bone at the back of her head, or would he have seen himself hanging, arms spread, not actually dancing, yet part of a huge dance?

"Weird!" he said aloud, now staring at the ceiling and running the short memory through his mind over and over again, as if he were editing film. He considered not only Jess's strange eyes, but also the brief, intruding reminder of his childish dream.

And at last his mother called him. The takeout had arrived. Roland swung himself up from his bed and made for the door, pausing as he caught a glimpse of himself in his mirror. There he was, tall, broad shouldered, a little gangly, but not too bad. His dark brown hair was worn as long as the Crichton dress code allowed, which was certainly not very long. It made him look rather more conservative than he really wanted to be, but Chris had streaked it a little for him, so that he seemed to have grown a comb of brassy gold. He couldn't help knowing that some people—his mother, of course (though she hardly counted), and Chris (because she had told him so)—thought he was handsome. All the same, he could never see it himself. Every time he confronted his reflection, he saw, yet again, the same old face, and he had no way of working out what it *really* looked like—except (of course) when he saw himself accidentally reflected in shop windows or in a photograph. Then he knew he looked very like his untrustworthy father, which might mean that somewhere along the line he, too, would walk away from everything and dissolve into the world out there, never to be found again. Roland cleared his throat and straightened himself, assuming at least the outer appearance of a trustworthy man.

Fabuloso! said his inner voice, praising his resolve, and he repeated it aloud, though once the exclamation was alive in the outside world, he found he didn't believe it. There was certainly nothing fabulous about him right then. Quite the reverse.

Hungry! He suddenly felt hungry. How could he possibly have so many troubles and still feel hungry? All the same, he welcomed the feeling. At least it proved there were some things in a shifting world that could be relied on.

Roland set off, pleased to have something to look forward to, but in the hall beyond his bedroom door he paused. The wall was hung with family pictures. There he was as a smiling baby, as a toddler, as a boy of nine, delighted with his birthday cake. There was a slightly blurred photograph of Martin in his stroller and one of Danny on a rocking horse. There was his mother with *her* mother, and there was an old photograph of grandparents from the other side of the family, his father's father looking back at him with a shy, sly smile, and his father's mother looking as if she did not trust the photographer and might be about to shout instructions. "I'm more than a match for you—more than a match for anyone," she seemed to be asserting. "Do as I tell you! I'm the boss!" She had a hand on her husband's shoulder, as if she were arresting him, while his son, Roland's father, stood a little apart from his parents like a meek servant. "Hi there, Dad!" Roland mumbled. He sometimes wondered if he didn't wear a similar cautious expression himself from time to time. Looking at that half-remembered pictured face, he thought that he and his father seemed rather like houses haunted by each other's ghost. It was not a comfortable thought. *Hungry!* he reminded himself. *I'm hungry!*

"'Childe Roland to the dark tower came,'" he said aloud, and laughed. Then he strode past the family portrait gallery, making for the dining room and for the mixed pleasures of food, family, and television.

SATURDAY

Saturday. Roland half woke not to the usual luxurious, relaxed, inner-weekend silence, but to the sound of a storm. It took him a minute to realize that the fierce wind and distant thunder were all inside his head. Once he had come to terms with this, he lay still for a while, trying to force a weekend feeling to emerge. After all, he didn't have to leap up, drag on his school uniform, and then argue with his mother over whether or not he would be late unless she let him drive to school in her car. On Saturdays he didn't have to point out to her, yet again, that his school was much farther away than her office block or that the bus, which stopped right outside their house, also stopped at the very door of that office. Saturday! Of course, he had assignments to do, but there would be time for all that, and time, too, to do his own thing—a bit of reading, a trek down to the park to play a round or two of tennis with Tom, and later to spend time with Chris. No! Of course, Chris was away for the weekend. Roland grimaced sleepily. Saturday's usual feelings of space and possibility were all in place, so why wasn't he at ease with the world?

Then, opening his eyes, he found he must have gone to sleep staring through darkness at the bottom drawer of his desk. It was the first thing he saw. So far, with his eyes tight shut, he'd been able to put off thinking about all that. But now—well, he had to face it, didn't he? After all, it was going to be part of every minute of the weekend ahead of him. Roland shrugged, closed his eyes again, and tried to settle more deeply into his bed. But there would be no comfort and ease on this particular Saturday morning. He might as well be up and doing.

It all progressed in a way that was utterly usual, though from time to time Roland caught himself feeling that he had been displaced and was watching himself from some other dimension, eating breakfast, exchanging a few ritual insults with Danny and Martin, and then helping his mother by loading the dishwasher and wiping the tabletop. He was watching his own hands as they touched, lifted, folded, opened drawers, and held cups of tea, almost believing that they belonged to someone else. Later he watched himself setting off with Danny and a friend from down the road to the park and the tennis club. Tom was waiting for them. There were often vacant courts at that time in the morning, and after all, it *was* autumn. Another two weeks and the club would be closing down until next spring. Tom and he slugged their way through a couple of sets, while that distant, observing self watched a little scornfully, knowing that though all this was actually happening, it was not what was *really* going on. Roland was simply filling in time until . . .

"Your serve!" yelled Tom.

Roland usually beat Tom. He was better at coming up to the net and angling his returns into inaccessible corners, whereas Tom definitely was a back-line man, with long, strong, but largely predictable strokes. However, today Roland was playing carelessly—or perhaps, he told himself (determined to be fair), Tom was playing particularly well. It was hard to say, but one way or another, though he was usually determined to win, this morning he didn't really care. In fact, he felt superior when Tom, though trying hard to be laid back about his victory, failed to hide his great delight. Later they sat, side by side, on a bank watching two courts at once. Danny was playing on one, and there was a particularly lively doubles match on the other. One of the doubles players hit a massive smash, and the few watchers gasped and whistled admiringly as they clapped for him.

"Now, there's style!" said a resonant but slightly lisping voice somewhere behind and above Roland's head—a familiar voice, he thought. He had certainly heard it before, had heard it long ago, but recently, too—somewhere on television, perhaps. Twisting a little, he tried to look casually at the man who had spoken, noting with a vague surprise that he was wearing a hat like a dark sombrero and a long black coat that seemed a strangely heavy garment, even on an autumn day. Looking up at him from below, Roland made out a thick neck, the underside of a slightly sagging jawline, nostrils, and the lower rim of a pair of sunglasses. There was a gasp from the crowd, and Roland glanced back at the game just in time to see that one of the doubles players at the nearer end of the court had hit a high lob. The two players on the far side of the net ran frantically inward, both concentrating on the ball and on nothing else. Colliding violently, they fell, spread-eagled on the court, to the accompaniment of mingling cries of sympathy and derision. *Fabuloso!* he thought as he clapped, irritated to find himself using, yet again, his father's insistent word.

"Fabuloso!" exclaimed that slightly lisping voice behind and above him.

Roland froze. He took a long, deliberate breath. Twisting a little, he looked again at the man standing behind him—not an easy thing to do when he had to peer not only backward but upward, too. The man was gazing at the court in a perfectly normal way for someone enjoying a tennis match. Roland, still looking up and back, could make out even less of him than he had the first time. He would have moved forward, but there was someone sitting directly in front of him. How could it possibly be a coincidence that such an odd word had been used at the very moment he was thinking it? Yet how could it possibly be anything else? For a fantastic moment he caught himself wondering if the man in the dark hat could possibly *be* his father, transformed and made into an entirely different man by plastic surgery, say—plastic surgery in Hong Kong or the Philippines. However, his father had certainly been tall, whereas the man in the dark hat seemed to be on the short side. Asking himself mad questions, Roland wriggled forward between the other tennis enthusiasts. Could height be altered by gifted plastic surgery? Could doctors chop a few inches out of somebody's shinbones, say? The concealment of unnaturally short legs might explain the necessity of a long black coat. But when he twisted around again, hoping to take another, more fruitful glance at the lisping stranger, he found there was open space behind him. The man had disappeared.

Roland and Danny trailed home to a standing lunch in the kitchen, after which Roland loaded the dishwasher and then, shutting his bedroom door firmly on all family life, collapsed onto his bed and into his current book—a thriller about many different sorts of treachery—until his mother banged on his door, telling him to get off his butt and put himself behind the lawn mower. Roland groaned loudly and theatrically but obeyed, feeling a certain relief, because somehow he needed to keep moving. All day his inner voice had been kept busy instructing him. *Yes! Do it.* Do one thing after the other—move calmly through the day until . . . (here dim feelings clarified alarmingly) . . . until the moment came when he would be free to grab his bike to shoot over to the shopping center. Once there, he would lock his bike into a bike stand and weave his way down that narrow alley to the Riverlaw Reserve, knocking, at last, on Jess Ferret's green door. Once he openly acknowledged these intentions, Roland's thoughts moved on, and he began puzzling as to why he should feel so determined to pay Jess Ferret a weekend visit.

Why not wait until next Monday? Why not find out about Jess in the familiar context of the school yard, where they were naturally brought together? She might not be quite so suspicious of him there, so why not? *Because Chris will be back by then,* Roland quickly answered himself, only to find that though this was a possible reason (and a sensible one too), it was not entirely the true answer. He was wanting to visit Jess today because he had grown *curious* about her. *Hang about a bit,* he cried inwardly, carefully mowing around an oleander as he did so. What on earth was there about Jess Ferret to catch anyone's attention? Was he planning to take her by surprise and see her eyes perform their odd intensifying trick once more, or was it simply that it annoyed him to remember how readily she had walked away from him without once looking back over her shoulder?

EDGING PAST MEDUSA

So, late in the afternoon Roland found himself standing in front of the green door and staring cautiously at a polished brass knocker—a head of Medusa, which looked back at him, eyes wide and mad under a coiffure of twining serpents, lips parted in a smile filled with enormous, shining teeth. Refusing to meet her blank, brazen gaze (for after all, you never know!), he seized the head and knocked loudly, half expecting the knocker to twist in his fingers and snap at him. A door somewhere beyond the green door opened and shut. Rapid thumping steps came closer and closer. Then the green door swung open, and Roland and Jess stood looking at each other with different sorts of astonishment.

"Not you again!" she exclaimed. "What on earth do you want?"

"Nice to see you, too," said Roland, so taken aback that he was relieved to find he had something to say. Seen here in her own house, late on a Saturday afternoon, Jess was somehow an entirely different proposition from the dull, familiar girl who had been sitting, year after year, halfway down a wide variety of classrooms. She had not become slender and elegant overnight; the pimple at her hairline still showed—he could even tell she had been squeezing it earlier in the day. All the same, it wouldn't have been exaggerating to say that Jess Ferret was glowing. Her hair stood out in a halo of darkness, and it suddenly occurred to Roland that this roughly cut black hair always made him expect brown eyes. It still came as a shock to him, even though he had looked *at* her and *over* her and *around* her for so many years, to encounter a strong, clear blue gaze. An odd, triumphant excitement shone in every part of her . . . not only in her eyes, but in the curve of her lips and the arch of her dark eyebrows. It even seemed to radiate from the very texture of her olive skin.

Of course, she wasn't wearing school uniform, which might have made some difference. QUANTUM LEAP, said the words on her T-shirt, naming a trendy band, which was yet another unexpected thing about Saturday's Jess Ferret. If he had ever thought about it, Roland would have imagined her choosing the sort of dim classical music that goes tinkling on and on without having any true beginning or ending. She was wearing blue jeans, as he was himself, and her feet were bare. Still, the transformation didn't lie in her clothes so much as in that new brightness that she seemed to be giving off like a sort of heat.

"Me again," he said, making both his voice and his smile confident and charming. Well, it often worked.

"Oh, Fairfield! Just get lost!" exclaimed Jess, shaking her head at him. All the same, she did not slam the door in his face. Roland believed he could make out the beginning of a reluctant grin hovering, faintly, at the outermost edges of her mouth.

"Where are your manners?" he asked reprovingly. "Go on! Ask me in, now I'm here."

"Bugger good manners!" Jess exclaimed. "I want the weekend to myself."

"The thing is," said Roland, "the more you say things like that, the nosier I become." He saw her blue eyes shift suddenly and begin staring over his shoulder. Turning, he saw the front garden of the house to the right was no longer empty. A neighbor with a long hoe had come into sight and was working down the long hedge line, apparently chopping shadows into the soil.

"Hello, Jessie," the neighbor called, obviously aware that she had been observed. She straightened, looking at Roland with unabashed curiosity. "How's your mum these days?" she asked cozily.

"Working too hard," Jess replied. "Traveling!"

"She's been away for a day or two, hasn't she?" the neighbor asked. "I hope she's making her fortune."

"She sounds pretty cheesed off when she calls up each

night," said Jess, and as she spoke her long fingers closed on Roland's wrist in an unexpectedly powerful grip. "Okay! In! Come on in," she mouthed, then smiled and waved past him at the neighbor. "See you later."

AN UNNATURAL STILLNESS

Roland stepped obediently over the threshold, only to find himself standing beside Jess in a long, dim hall. At first he believed they had an audience—that there was a line of people just inside the door, all flattened back against the wall and staring out at them in utter silence. Then he saw that this deputation of tall, veiled figures was really a series of coats hanging from hooks, with hats in a line above them, and boots and shoes in a line below. A narrow ledge of dark-stained wood, not wide enough to be called a shelf, ran above this row of hooks and all around the hall. To his left, a little ahead of where they were standing, he saw a door, slightly ajar, and then a hall table, on which stood a big vase of flowers. Beyond that a narrow staircase mounted to a shadowy landing and an upper story. The hall led on past the staircase and past a second door (this time on the right and also partly open) to a third door (closed), which Roland guessed might open into some sort of kitchen. Embraced by a strange, still, and disconcerting grandeur, he stood staring around him, trying to work out just what there was about Jess Ferret's house that was causing the hairs on the back of his neck to prickle defensively. There was nothing dangerous to be seen, yet Roland felt he was in danger.

"Come on, then!" ordered Jess in tones of irritated resignation. "You've only got this far because I didn't want to argue with you while Mrs. Ross was listening. I'll make you a cup of coffee. And then you can bugger off."

"Gee, I can tell you've been to charm school," said Roland.

"Actually, I was born charming," Jess replied, leading him down the hall. "It's genetic. Gene number seven on chromosome forty-nine."

What was there about this house that was so chilling? It was as if he had stepped into a strange and frightening freak show, and yet there was not a single thing he could see or name that wasn't, when he looked at it directly, entirely predictable. Through the door on his left he had a sliding glimpse of a sitting room lined with bookshelves and leather couches and chairs—elegant but quite ordinary. It was true, though, that the door to the right opened on something unexpected. He glimpsed a workbench, on which a microscope sat in front of a rack of test tubes, with glass beakers and bottles to either side. He had the impression of books stretching from floor to ceiling before he was hurried past. But after all, Jess's father was some sort of scientist. Perhaps a private laboratory wasn't so very surprising. And now Jess was opening the third door and leading the way—sure enough—into a kitchen. It was much bigger than Roland had expected it to be, and smelled of flowers. There was a vase of late roses at one end of the table, another mixed bouquet on top of the refrigerator, and a tiny, bright posy acting as a bookend on a shelf full of very old recipe books. Granny's recipes, perhaps! By now he was certain that he had walked in on something secret, without having any real reason for thinking so, or the least idea of what the secret might be. It was not as if he was either hearing or seeing the secret, he was simply breathing it in.

What he *was* able to see, however, was the new Jess Ferret . . . Jess Ferret transformed. That defiant elation, tangible from the moment she had opened the door, was burning through and through her, and Roland couldn't flatter himself it was because he had turned up on her doormat, grinning.

"Sit down," she ordered, swinging one end of a wooden bench out from under the kitchen table. Roland meekly obeyed, and as he did so his drifting impressions locked together and he began to take mental notes, just as though he might have to sit a Jess Ferret test later in the day.

All the things he had seen so far—the carpet, the doors, the refrigerator, and so on—were just what you would expect to see in any home, so why was he feeling uneasy? Why did this whole house seem to be set at an odd angle to the rest of the world? Why did he feel that the answers to these questions would be so alarming that it was wiser, perhaps, not to ask them, not even in the shadowy, silent room of his own head?

Everything was tidy. But then, his own home, when he had left it, was tidy enough—tidy for a Saturday, that is. After all, hadn't he himself helped to tidy it? But *his* home had a constantly changing surface. Within ten minutes or so disorder automatically began to assert itself. A continual shiver of change ran through all the rooms in Roland's house, and he knew there was some scientific name for the way things constantly broke apart and fell into disorder. Entropy! That was it. It was part of the nature of the world. But there was no such natural shivering in Jess's home. It was as if the flowers in the vases would never fade, the books on the shelves would never be taken down, as if every single thing around Jess were fixed forever.

"Is your mum really at work?" he asked casually.

"They both are," she replied. "Both parents, that is. They enjoy working and they both flog themselves. I spend a lot of time on my own, which suits me just fine. I keep telling you that."

"Well, I could say I don't want to push in," said Roland, "but, really, I do. It's like I said yesterday. Out of the blue I felt curious about a few people, and you were one of them. It's a compliment, really," he added, half believing it himself for a moment. But Jess snorted, grinding coffee as she snorted. And there was even something odd about this simple, everyday action. Roland felt as if he were watching a haunting of some kind, though Jess's moving arm seemed completely real, and there was nothing in the least transparent about either her or the wall behind her.

"So!" she said. "You've got all nosy about me for some reason, and you thought I'd fall at your feet just with the flattery of being seen—the battery of fleeing scene," she added, more to herself than to Roland, as if she were testing her own nonsense for unexpected meanings. "Dream on, Fairfield! I'd rather flee the scene, and the battery of the flattery, too."

"Why do you do that?" asked Roland curiously.

"Do what?" she asked, turning with a small measuring cup of ground coffee in her hand.

"Twist words around," he replied.

"I like trying them out in different ways," Jess said. "I like spoonerisms . . . named after the Reverend Mr. Spooner, who used to do it by accident. Sometimes—not always, but sometimes—you come across great surprises and hidden jokes and meanings." Suspicion vanished from her voice as she said this.

But it quickly returned. "Not that you'd be interested in hidden meanings," she added.

Roland was surprised at how irritated her scorn made him feel. *Don't worry!* he thought of saying. *If I weren't being blackmailed, I wouldn't be checking you out.* He shot a furtive look at his watch. This time last weekend he and Chris had been sitting side by side, half watching a five o'clock film together. It had been funny, and they both had been laughing, and as they laughed her hand had been holding *his* hand against her right breast, and his nose had been drawing in *her* scent. Sex and laughter were mixed up in his mind whenever he remembered it. And here he was, only a week later, struggling to flirt his way into some sort of relationship with Jess Ferret. *I don't have to bother with this,* he thought, and found he was on the point of standing up and stalking out. But then, quite unexpectedly, he found himself laughing at the madness of it all, and at himself, too. Jess looked almost startled. Laughter was apparently the last thing she had expected. Her own face became brighter and lighter, and she started laughing with him. *I've won,* thought Roland, without knowing quite what it was he had won. *We might get on together after all.* For Jess's laughing face, looking back at him from the heart of this curious, dead kitchen, was both warm and funny. She put the ground coffee in a French press, carefully poured boiling water in on it, then stepped back and sat down at the far end of the table.

"Just make polite conversation and we'll see where we go from there," she suggested.

"Does it have to be polite?" Roland asked.

"Begin with polite and we'll see what happens next," Jess said. "And I'm quite well, thank you, so don't bother asking me."

"You're making it hard for me," he complained. "That's two thirds of polite conversation just wiped away."

Jess's reply was once again unexpected, but different from all the other unexpected things she had said so far.

"The mad thing is that I can't help being flattered, in a way," she said, "and I feel really pissed off with myself just for *being* flattered. Not that I expect you to understand that," she added.

"Hey!" said Roland, clapping his hand to his chest. "I've got brain cells. I'm doing scholarship this year. I can understand great, long words with two syllables and all that."

Jess's grin, which had been fading, stretched out again. She rolled her eyes, then looked toward the coffeemaker as if it might have a useful comment to make. Roland looked at it too, a little apprehensively, but it had nothing to say.

"I just thought I had a mind above all that stuff," Jess said.

"What stuff?" asked Roland.

"Being impressed with clever, show-off types like you," she said, and made a face.

"Well, you're clever enough yourself—at math and science, that is," said Roland a little feebly, because her smile was reminding him of the Cheshire Cat's long grin.

"I am, aren't I?" she agreed. "Actually, I could probably do even better," she went on half boastfully, "but . . ." And then she broke off, stood up, and moved restlessly toward the kitchen sink.

"So why don't you?" asked Roland. "Do even better, I mean."

A cautious look crept over Jess's face, as if she was already regretting what she had said and was trying to work out a way of pulling her words back and swallowing them once more.

"Oh, I probably couldn't," she said at last. "I was probably making it up. I make things up all the time. Don't trust anything *I* say."

"Why are you trying to *hide* yourself?" asked Roland accusingly. "God! I'm nothing to hide from."

"I keep telling you," she said. "Telling you, and yelling, too! I don't want to be seen."

"Yes, *but*! Face it! You're *not* invisible," Roland replied, reasonably enough. "You're out and about, right? Anyone can see you."

Including Mr. Hudson! he was thinking to himself. *He's seen something about her. Something I'm missing out on. Because, right now, if anyone looks as if they're in charge of life, Jess Ferret does.*

And as he thought this the eerie feeling he had experienced from the moment he walked into Jess's house seemed to beat in on him, coming not only from Jess (now pouring coffee in the most straightforward way), but from the kitchen walls, the kitchen sink, the door of the refrigerator, and the shelves of books. The house seemed to be asserting itself over and over again in the same instant of time. *Here! Here! Here I am! This is what I am! This! This!*

Jess passed him a mug of coffee, then sat down at the other end of the table with a mug of her own.

"Nice house," he said, making polite conversation.

"You don't really think so," said Jess immediately. "I saw you looking around it a moment ago, and people who think something is nice don't look the way you did."

"I think it's wonderful," Roland said, which was close enough to the truth. "But sort of ghostly," he added. "Not that

I mind ghosts," he quickly added again. An odd look swept across Jess's face. He had seen that expression on many other faces before and recognized it immediately. Almost against her will Jess Ferret was going to boast about something.

"It's *my* house," she said. "I don't just mean that I live here. I mean that it belongs to me." It was her turn to add something. "And that ghostliness you're feeling is *my* ghostliness." It wasn't a question, and yet she looked across the table at him as if she were testing him with a riddle.

"Your house?" exclaimed Roland, genuinely surprised. Her challenge was working.

"Well, my parents separated," she explained. Roland bit himself back into silence, anxious not to divert her. "One of those *civilized* separations," Jess went on, mocking her absent parents this time rather than Roland. "And they did something that I've never heard of anyone else doing. They put the house in a trust in *my* name. So I *own* this house. Me, myself! You know how most people with separated parents get swapped around—three and a half days at Mum's apartment, then three and a half days with Dad and his new girlfriend, or whatever. Well, *my* pair shot off in their own directions, but they come turn and turn about to live with me in *my* house. I've always lived here. I was even born up there." Jess pointed at the ceiling. "I just love the feeling of actually owning it all. I don't know anyone else at school who lives in a house that actually belongs to them, do you?"

Roland shook his head.

"So even if you and your gang call me Weaselly, I'm really more in charge of my own life than any of you, and I like looking around at everyone else and secretly thinking the rest of you don't *know* me or anything about me." And Roland was certainly feeling an unexpected respect that was close to envy edging into his expression. "I just thought I'd mention it," said Jess. "Perhaps it's being owned by me that gives the house a spooky feeling. Perhaps I'm a . . . a creature of power." Roland had the uneasy feeling that she was laughing at him, and the possibility of being secretly laughed at by Jess Ferret disconcerted him.

"Well, lucky you," he said at last, glad to hear that his voice in the outside world was able to sound just as mocking as Jess Ferret's. Then he took his first sip of coffee and changed the subject to school gossip—something they could joke about together, which was what they did, talking after the first few minutes almost like friends. Later Roland found himself complaining about his brothers and listing their annoying habits. And then, remembering something, he dipped into his pocket and brought out the game of *Viper,* which he had transferred from his blazer to his windbreaker earlier in the day, anxious to frustrate any fraternal searching of his room.

"It's quite good fun," he told Jess, but found, a moment later, that no matter how cunningly he pushed its buttons, the game had stopped working.

"Flat batteries," said Jess.

"No," said Roland. "The batteries are new." He glanced around at the kitchen with reborn suspicion. Then he looked over at Jess and opened his mouth, not knowing quite what he was going to say next. Perhaps she anticipated some awkward question, for she leaped to her feet and turned to check the coffee. The pot was empty. It was a natural time for him to go.

Roland now realized that, for all the curious feelings of arrested space in Jess's strange house, he had also been haunted by the feeling as they talked that something else was happening. Was it possible he had been hearing footsteps, not upstairs or out in the hall, but right next to his ears, as if the sound were structured into the air around him? Yet, whenever he had tried to listen properly, there had been no sound—no vibration—except the pulse of his own intrusive heartbeat. Certainly whenever he talked and Jess listened, the room around him seemed to reject his voice, and his words rolled away from its surfaces like raindrops rolling off plastic. So he was relieved that the coffee pot was empty and it was time for him to go. After all, simply by getting into this house and laughing and talking with Jess at the other end of the table, he had won half a victory. Besides, to his surprise he found he enjoyed her dry, sly way of laughing and the shrewd and funny things she had to say about other people in their class. Rather uncomfortably, Roland found he could imagine her parodying Chris and himself to someone else. And she was also a reader. She had read some of the same books he had—not just the books assigned at school, but detective stories as well as a bit of lively trash. Thinking of this, he reached out idly toward a book lying on the table, but Jess leaned forward and swept it from under his curious fingers.

"My secret!" she said.

"Why? Is it pornographic or something?" Roland asked.

"Yes," she said, nodding vigorously. "Far too far out for a nice boy like you."

It was an old book bound in black—probably withdrawn from a library, for he could see a Dewey decimal number on its spine: 540.1, he read, committing the number to memory. After all, it might be a useful clue to something. And then, glancing up at the rows of cookbooks on the shelf beside the stove, he was suddenly sure that none of them was a cookbook. Looking at them with true attention, he could see that the faint marks up and down their spines were not familiar print, but tattered hieroglyphics, emblems, and perforated patterns.

"How about I come around tomorrow?" he suggested. "Unless you're planning to spend the whole day in church or something?"

But Jess, following his gaze, had seen him notice the books, and grew suddenly defensive. He felt her close up once more.

"How about you don't," she said. "I'm taking an oath of silence. You'd only be wasting your time, when you could be out tasting your wine. And that could be *whine*—with an *h,* by the way," she added, almost to herself. "Grizzlers often seem to be tasting their own whines, don't they?"

"Be fair! I'm not a grizzler," said Roland stiffly.

"No, it doesn't apply to you," agreed Jess. "But you never know what the words are suddenly going to reveal when you toss them round. It's always worth trying them out."

Walking through the hall, Roland suddenly stopped.

"What's wrong?" asked Jess.

"I've left that game of *Viper* on the table," he said. "I need it to bribe my brothers when I'm at home." He turned back toward the kitchen.

"I'll get it," cried Jess, spinning around and making for the kitchen door as if, having got him this far, she was anxious to keep him safely in the hall. Left on his own for a moment, Roland glanced toward the front door, nodding mockingly at the line of ghostly coats and boots. Then he glanced toward the top of the stairs.

It was an autumn evening and the landing was darkening. All the same, he could make out a figure standing in the concealing shadows and looking down at him. At first it stood unnaturally still, and then it seemed to fluctuate, as if it were somehow painted on the air and must billow a little whenever doors were opened or shut. As Roland thought this the kitchen door did open, catching him in a shaft of light. He turned away quickly as Jess came toward him. Even though she seemed to bring her own light with her, the briefly dismissed shadows returned to the hall.

"My parents will be home at any moment," Jess was saying as she came toward him. "I'd better get dinner on the way."

"Good cook, are you?" asked Roland, simply for the sake of saying something. He was not in the least interested whether Jess Ferret could cook or not and certainly did not believe she needed to make dinner for her parents. At that moment he found it hard to believe she had any parents at all.

Jess thrust his game of *Viper* toward him, then walked on to fling the front door wide open. Stepping out onto the porch, Roland turned, shooting an apparently casual glance over Jess's shoulder as he did so. There was no one and nothing on the landing. All the same, a moment earlier he had seen—he had seen—he *knew* he had seen . . .

And then he was outside, not exactly pushed out, but guided through the door in a fashion so determined that he could not resist. "Good-bye," Jess was saying, wiggling her fingers at him and smiling a little mockingly as she closed the door on any farewells he might be planning. There was nothing to do but stroll back across the footbridge to his tethered bike and make for home.

Streetlights were already on, but there were quite a few people strolling on the riverbanks—people who were enjoying the autumnal twilight and the reflections in the water. It wasn't deserted.

"Beautiful evening," said a man's voice. "Don't you think so?"

"Great," agreed Roland, nodding but not bothering to see who had spoken. After all, strangers walking on riverbanks continually commented on the weather to one another. Weather was one of the things that everyone had in common. And it really was a beautiful evening in the Riverlaw Reserve—mellow and gentle. Then it occurred to him that there was something familiar about the voice, and he looked around quickly, though he couldn't pick out just which passerby had spoken to him. But right then he was not interested in any casual conversation. Indeed, Roland found to his surprise that he was actually trembling a little. He had not been able to tell if that shadowy figure he had glimpsed at the top of the stairs was male or female, but he was sure it had been . . . not transparent, exactly, but not quite solid, either. And he felt, disconcertingly, that what he had seen—or at any rate, had half seen—was another version, a distorted ghost, of Jess Ferret herself.

As he made for the alley between the riverbank and the main road the breathing began. He had never heard it so loudly or clearly before. Something was flowing; something was being exchanged; something was falling apart; something was putting itself together. *Careful,* said his cautioning inner voice. *Back! Stand back.*

Roland took a breath of his own, released it softly, and concentrated on taking this advice—on being careful, and stepping away as he did so. Slowly that breathing gave way to silence, then fell away altogether. The sound of the main road traffic, along with the murmuring of distant voices, burst in on him, and everything became normal once again. All the same, he was sure that though he had managed to close himself off from it, the breathing was still going on, braiding itself through the evening air and waiting to break in on him once more.

When he reached the mouth of the alley, he came to an abrupt standstill, jerked out of his thoughts of Jess Ferret by something entirely different that had just occurred to him. Tennis courts. The man at the tennis courts. The one with the slightly lisping voice who had exclaimed, "Fabuloso!" at the very moment that Roland himself had been thinking it. It was that same voice that had commented on the beauty of the evening. Roland spun around to look right and left along the riverbank behind him. Evening strollers were moving like shadows under the willows. There was no way he would ever be able to tell which of them had spoken to him in that familiar voice, or even if the speaker was still in sight. There was nothing he could do but reclaim his bike and, after putting on his helmet like a good Crichton prefect, pedal his way home.

Reporting In

"Good beginning!" declared Mr. Hudson heartily. Roland wondered if this heartiness was quite what it was trying to be. "At least you're talking to her. Good! Now, how did she seem? Upset in any way?"

"No," said Roland, making himself sound puzzled at the

mere idea of Jess Ferret being upset in any way. "Actually," he added, thinking it would do no harm to mention at least one of his impressions (though he had every intention of keeping most of them to himself), "she seemed a lot brighter than she usually does at school. Not that I *know* how she usually is," he added as quickly as he could. "We don't hang out together."

"Oh, I think our Jess keeps herself to herself," said Mr. Hudson rather cozily. "If she does talk to anyone, it's probably to keep them at a distance. Odd, when you come to think of it. Most talk is intended to bring people closer, isn't it?" He hesitated; his eyebrows arched delicately. "Was her mother surprised when you turned up on her doorstep?"

"Her parents were at work," Roland said, and then wished he hadn't said this. What else could he have said, though? After all, it was only what he had been told.

He knew immediately that this snippet interested Mr. Hudson in what seemed to be a disproportionate way. The same betraying excitement that Roland had glimpsed on Friday came and went before Mr. Hudson could prevent it. And Roland not only saw it again now, but also saw Mr. Hudson struggling to iron it out of existence—too late, as it happened, because by then Roland knew for certain that whatever was generating Mr. Hudson's keenest interest was certainly not concern about Jess. What Mr. Hudson *most* wanted to know about had to do with the presence or the absence of her parents.

"What? Both of them at work?" he exclaimed, arching his lively eyebrows. Looking just above Mr. Hudson's eyes, Roland watched those eyebrows in case they signaled some message against their owner's wishes—some clue as to what was really going on. Mr. Hudson deliberately used them to close off a topic or ask questions across a crowded room. But his eyebrows had a life of their own, one he could not entirely control, and they might hint at things that Mr. Hudson would rather keep to himself. "Her father is overseas at present," he went on in a meditative voice. "Well, perhaps that was what she meant by saying he was at work. I believe her parents have been separated for some time. I, er, take it there was no sign of her *mother*?"

"Sign?" repeated Roland blankly, still suspicious of something without quite knowing what. "She wasn't there, sir."

"But she could have left some evidence of her existence," insisted Mr. Hudson. "Knitting on a chair? A shopping bag? I don't know," he said irritably. "Some proof that she is living in that house." Images of the Riverlaw kitchen flooded through Roland and, oddly enough, put him in touch with the strange, arrested atmosphere of Jess Ferret's house. He remembered how it had seemed on Saturday, that though Jess might grind coffee, then plunge it and pour it, the kitchen, once it was unobserved, would go back to being exactly what it had been before these acts had taken place. Well, there had certainly been no sign of any mother in *that* kitchen. In a way, he thought, there had been no sign of anybody, not even of Jess, for all that she had been standing directly in front of him. However, he didn't mention any of these impressions to Mr. Hudson, but simply sighed a little and puffed out his cheeks, looking nonplussed as he did so (something it was all too easy to do).

"Did Jess *say* anything about her mother?" Mr. Hudson persisted.

"She said her parents were at work, that's all," Roland repeated, beginning to feel treacherous. And perhaps something of this showed in his face, for Mr. Hudson's eyebrows relaxed a little, and Mr. Hudson smiled at him.

"I know this must be confusing for you," he said, "but I really am *worried* about Jess, and I don't know how official to be about my worry. Naturally, I don't want to poke my nose into anyone's life outside school. Private life is private life. I do believe that most devoutly. But I don't want to stand back, saying that it's none of my business, if there's something seriously wrong and there's a chance that I might be able to help."

"How long do I have to keep spying on her?" asked Roland restlessly.

"Oh, I wouldn't call it *spying,*" said Mr. Hudson. "Not *spying,* exactly. Let's call it checking up. Anyhow, I just don't know the answer to that one. In some ways I'm all at sea myself. Let's just run a week of . . . of observation, eh? Then we might give up. Anyhow, off you go. And Roland!" he added as Roland was about to leave the room. "Thanks!" said Mr. Hudson warmly. "After all this complication, I do hope you enjoy your lunch when you finally get to it. Hope there are some nice surprises in it."

"There won't be," said Roland. "I made it myself. Made lunch for my brothers, too." It was uncomfortable to be thanked as if he were doing something out of true concern, particularly when he was keeping his strangest and most important impressions to himself. Was his secrecy a form of revenge, or did he feel somehow loyal to Jess, because, after all, she was his age and in his class, and (after all, again) she *had* made him a mug of coffee? He had certainly not mentioned (here he found his breath quickening a little) the figure he had glimpsed at the top of the stairs looking down at him, but then, why should he? Whatever it might have been, it was not Jess's mother.

"Brothers!" Mr. Hudson was exclaiming with a new wry sincerity. "Believe me, I know how it is. . . . I still run around after mine, and he's a grown man."

"We see him on television, sir," said Roland, and as he heard the ghost of their old teacher-pupil fellowship haunting his voice he knew he was pretending. Their future friendship had fallen away before it truly existed—and now it was gone, Roland felt sure, forever.

ALCHEMY

Roland stepped out into sunshine only to be filled with relief at finding himself part of the familiar life of the school lunch hour. He put Mr. Hudson, together with his questions and arching eyebrows, firmly behind him. There, on the seats outside the school library, was *his* crowd—Tom, Stephen, Shelley, and Chris. Chris saw him coming toward them and waved a half-eaten roll at him, somehow managing to make this ordinary action seem both funny and alluring.

"So!" she cried as he sat down beside her under the library windows and began to unpack his lunch. "Go on! We've got a chance to talk for twenty minutes. Tell me everything. Did you have a great weekend without me?" She sounded perfectly certain, nevertheless, that this must have been impossible.

"Oh, sure!" said Roland. "Parties, parties, parties!"

Chris punched his arm. She was being playful, but she actually hurt him.

"Okay! Okay! What did you *really* do?" she demanded.

"Saturday I played tennis. Sunday I went to listen to Quantum Leap," said Roland, quickly naming the band whose name had leaped out at him from Jess's Saturday T-shirt. "They were doing an open-air gig in the park, so I wandered over and ended up sharing a Coke and muffins with Jess Ferret." He thought he should mention Jess in case, later on, he accidentally referred to her in some way.

"What? The Weasel?" asked Chris. "You really must have been desperate."

Chris was not being spiteful. She was using an offhand name that people had called Jess for years and years. You couldn't have a name like Ferret, after all, without having jokes made about it, and Jess had always responded in a vaguely good-natured way when people used it in her hearing. But then, even when people called her by her real name, Jess had a trick of looking around as if she thought they might be talking to someone else. On Friday, Roland would not have thought twice about hearing her called "the Weasel." Now, however, he felt treacherous for the second time in a single lunch hour, this time because he did not challenge Jess's nickname.

"Of course, Dad, my darling old man, was very frisky . . . ," Chris was saying.

Roland listened vaguely, staring past her toward Jess's linden tree. She was sitting on the grass beneath it, skirt pulled over her knees and a book propped in her lap. There was the usual crowd of people walking and wheeling around her, and yet today she stood out from them all, etched against the tree trunk behind her as if she were outlined with a thin thread of light. Roland blinked and the thread of light vanished. Just for a moment he had been distracted by a trick of his own.

And now, as he studied Jess this Monday morning, all sorts of thoughts began to race around his head, like pet shop mice on a wheel. After months and even years of being mostly honest he had, suddenly (over the last three days), become addicted to lying—well, to saying things that were only half true, anyway. He had been acting out a self that was not his true self, stretching the meaning of words so far it was a wonder they did not spring back and sting him. Sometimes when the right word had presented itself, he had looked past it, pretending it wasn't there. Funnily enough, though, some of the twisting lies he had told Jess Ferret had trapped him by suddenly becoming true. Last Friday, for example, he had pretended an interest in her because though they had shared a series of classrooms over the years, they were still virtual strangers. But on Saturday night he had enjoyed her company in a way he had never anticipated, and even though their gossiping over coffee had been guarded, and despite the fact that she had turned him out of her house so very efficiently, he believed she had enjoyed being with him. The interest he had pretended in the beginning had turned on him and trapped him by becoming real. He could feel it working in him at that very moment.

"You're not listening to me," Chris shouted accusingly. "I'm telling you about my weekend—la, la, la—and you're staring into space."

"I *was* listening," said Roland—yet another half-truth, for even though the sound of Chris's voice had filled his ears, he hadn't heard a word she had been saying. Fixing his eyes on her, he saw she was looking around the school yard and frowning a little as she tried to work out just what it was that had stolen his attention away from her. But, of course, from Chris's point of view there was nothing to see. Old Weaselly-Ferret was perfectly visible there in the middle distance, along with a whole lot of other people, but she would be no more meaningful to Chris than grass or trees, or the west end of the football field . . . probably less so.

"I'm not going over it all again," Chris declared a little petulantly. "I was telling you about the local guys. But if we happen to meet up with any of them anywhere, I'll point one out and you can question him about what I got up to."

She emphasized the word *him* slightly, but it was the words *point* and *one* that began chasing each other through Roland's mind, for they suddenly reminded him of the book Jess had snatched away from him as his Saturday visit was coming to a close. The number on its spine flashed through his mind like a little vision, luminous and golden. He remembered those other books too, all marked with symbols rather than properly legible titles. Even if they turned out, after all, to be cookbooks, he felt he would not want to eat anything made from any recipes those books might contain. So later, when he and Chris went into the library, he looked first on the shelves and then in the computer catalog for any books that might be classified under 540.1, but could not find one.

Roland, however, knew the library well. He had helped out with shelving before graduating to work behind the checkout desk. He and Chris had actually exchanged their first kisses in the back room between shelves crowded with new books waiting to be processed and those filled with battered books waiting to be mended. There, beside the checkout desk, on the bottom shelf of the reference section, sat the fat volumes of

Dewey decimal classification, and confidently squatting, Roland hauled one out and thumbed his way to the five hundreds, which he already knew represented pure science. As it turned out, the number 540.1 stood for a category that was dubiously scientific. It was halfway to being witchcraft. The number 540.1 was a classification number for alchemy. *Al-chem-y!* The word sounded in his mind like the tolling of a bell. He knew that alchemists had searched for a formula to turn base metals into gold. But there might be more to alchemy than that. After considering this thoughtfully, he replaced the Dewey decimal classification volume and pulled out an adjacent dictionary, searched its pages, and in due course began to read.

DEFINITIONS

Alchemy (AL-ka-me) *n* 1. A combination of chemistry, magic, and philosophy studied in the Middle Ages. Alchemy tried to find or prepare substances that would turn cheaper metals into gold and silver, and that would also cure any human ailment and prolong human life. In its fullest sense alchemy was a philosophical system containing a complex and rudimentary science, elaborated with astrology, religion, mysticism, magic, theosophy, and many other constituents. Alchemy dealt not only with the mysteries of matter, but also with those of creation and life. It sought to harmonize the human individual with the universe surrounding him. 2. *Figurative:* a magical or mysterious power of transforming one thing into another (*The lovely alchemy of spring*).

THE FLICKER IN MR. HUDSON'S EYES

"Jess reads books on alchemy," Roland told Mr. Hudson, reporting in two days later at midmorning break. He made this sound as if it were something he had only just discovered. And as he said it he caught, yet again, that sudden, avid flicker in Mr. Hudson's eyes before Mr. Hudson quickly looked down, pretending to straighten a pile of papers.

Gotcha! Roland thought triumphantly, and continued watching slyly until Mr. Hudson looked back up again.

"What does her mother have to say to that?" he asked lightly.

"Nothing much," said Roland, shrugging. "Well, not as far as I know."

"You have met her mother by now?" asked Mr. Hudson even more casually, as if it were a question well and truly off to one side.

"She works late," said Roland, not letting on that he had not spoken to Jess since Saturday night.

"So you haven't actually met her mother yet?" insisted Mr. Hudson.

Roland was forced to admit that he had not.

"And Jess still hasn't said anything to you—anything to suggest that she's in trouble of any kind, that she's unhappy about anything?" persisted Mr. Hudson. "She hasn't confided in you in any way?"

"We've only just started talking to each other," Roland said as indignantly as he dared. "Sir, she's not going to pour her heart out to me in a day or two."

"Oh, you never know," said Mr. Hudson in a jolly, joking

voice. "You're supposed to have a way with words. Girls, too! That's why I chose you."

It isn't, thought Roland crossly. *You chose me because you could force me to chase after Jess Ferret whether I wanted to or not.*

A few more comments and he was free to walk away, pretending to be what he had been this time last week. *There is something going on there . . . something peculiar,* he was thinking.

Careful, muttered his instructing inner voice urgently. *Trickery! Trickery!*

Yet, in spite of its dedicated instruction he found, as he drove home, that he had not only turned into the road that led past the mall, but was actually turning into the mall parking lot, as well.

What's going on? he wondered, amazed at himself. *What am I doing here? I've reported in today. Hudson won't expect anything from me tomorrow. I don't have to visit Jess Ferret for a day or two.* All the same, there he was, parking his mother's car and feeling that he was not the person who had made the decisions that had brought him there. Someone *else* had been steering the car for him. Someone else, ignoring the promptings of that sensible inner voice, was crossing the road in front of the blue-and-silver café and the arched mall entrance. Someone *else* was now walking down the narrow lane to Riverlaw Reserve. Either that or he was a puppet, jerked around by wishes so deeply disguised that he could not put a name to them.

DREAM OR MEMORY

As he walked down the alley the sound of many voices came to meet him. All the same, he was astonished to find Riverlaw

Reserve crowded with people. Then he remembered. It was Wednesday. The Riverlaw Kindergarten Fund-raising Fair was in the process of folding itself away. There were still a few tents standing, though one of them subsided with a defeated, billowing sigh as he walked past. Two gallant fathers were still spinning a chocolate wheel, determined that the last boxes of chocolates (probably old stock donated by the supermarket) should go to good homes. A van, parked at a slight angle, its back doors open, still displayed a few items of secondhand clothing. He heard a group of women, anxious by now to head for home, discussing what to do next.

"We could bundle it up for the Salvation Army," one of them was saying.

"I don't think we should patronize them with stuff like this," said a second woman doubtfully. "I think we should just toss it out."

"It's been a good turnout for a Wednesday," another voice chimed in. "I wanted a Friday, but I don't think we'd have done any better."

"People do stock up for the weekend on a Friday, but then they've run out by midweek," remarked the first speaker. "Wednesday's undervalued."

Beyond the secondhand-clothes van there was yet another small tent—one Roland had not noticed to begin with. He eyed it casually, then stopped so abruptly that his teeth chattered with the impact.

QUANDO THE MAGICIAN, said the painted sign over the door of the tent. LAST SESSION, announced the words chalked on a blackboard standing at the tent doorway. The world darkened and retreated. Roland's ancient dream seemed to well up out of his memory, every detail in place, and to enclose his ringing head in a mask of iron.

"It *was* a dream," he whispered, or thought he whispered. In fact, he must have cried it aloud, for people turned to look at him. *It must have been a dream,* he added, silently this time, speaking into the echoing room of his own skull, which felt as if it were being forced to change shape, making him weak and dizzy as it did so. Was it actually painful—that change? Afterward, he felt that it must have been. He even imagined that he might have fainted without falling.

But the world came firmly into existence once more, and as he branched back into it he found his intentions had altered. In spite of his irritation with himself he had been planning to call on Jess. Now it seemed to him that he must have been summoned back to Riverlaw Reserve because Quando had whistled to him, even though he had not known, until this moment, that Quando was a real person. And now he also began to feel as if he must have planned this encounter from the beginning without letting anyone know he was planning it—not even himself. That was nonsense—it just had to be nonsense. Yet nonsense or not, didn't it have a natural connection with all the other things that had been going on in his life over the last few days? Wasn't it part of his argument with Chris earlier in the day, part of calling on Jess in her strange, still house, part of Mr. Hudson's blackmail, too, and possibly part of the impulse that had led him to steal the pens, the pie, and the notebook in the first place? And now, for the first time, it rushed in on him that the pens, the notebook, and the pie somehow paralleled that old gift of his dream—the gift of six felt pens, a coloring book, and a bar of chocolate. Yet if the magician was a real man, the gift must have been real too. *Chill out!* he commanded himself. *Pull yourself together! This just has to be a coincidence—an accident—it has to be rubbish.* Sternly instructing himself in this way, yet feeling completely certain that there was a true connection, Roland continued to stare at the name on the tent. Quando the Magician. There was no way out of it. He could not shrug his shoulders and walk past.

Roland paid three dollars to the woman sitting at the tent doorway.

"You'll love it," she promised him. "He's amazing."

Though it was late in the afternoon, there were quite a number of people, mostly mothers and little children, seated on white plastic chairs and staring with placid expectation toward a square of grass fenced in by colored cords that swooped, shining, between silver pegs. A small table was set slightly to one side of this grassy stage, while dominating the middle of the green (Roland took a shuddering breath) was a long box shaped like a coffin, held upright and tilted back in a supporting frame. And then, before he had any chance of coming to terms with this further icon of his childish memory, a man, resplendent in a swishing black cloak, a black crown set firmly on a wig of long black braids, swept in. The face between the braids was masked by thick white paint. He struck a dramatic attitude, then leaped into the expectant green square, where he stood, ginger brown eyes staring out of nothingness, gazing around at them all.

"Ta-DAH!" he cried, mocking the drama of his own entrance.

It was the Quando of his dreams, no doubt about it—older (well, he must be older, though it was impossible to tell), and made somehow more potent by blankness. And at the same time Roland knew immediately that this magician in the swinging cloak was the same black-coated man who had stood behind him crying, "Fabuloso!" during the tennis match, and that his voice was the same cultured and slightly lisping voice that had praised the evening on Saturday night.

Fabuloso! he had thought, and "Fabuloso!" the man in the black coat had said aloud, almost as if the word had flown out of Roland's head, only to be snatched from the air by a stranger, then uttered in the stranger's voice.

"Now, my friends," Quando was saying to his audience, "I don't want you to think that I am one of those new-age fools who believes in magic. I promise you that everything I do is pure trickery. Watch me closely and you'll soon see through all my little deceits." As he spoke he snapped his fingers, and his hand suddenly filled with a fan of big, bright cards rimmed with gold. He stared at them as if he were more surprised than anyone else to find them there, and then, as everybody laughed, he began to shuffle them with an easy grace before launching into a series of tricks—the sorts of tricks that, though they were totally inexplicable, you might expect any competent magician to perform. As he talked, with scarcely a pause, his eyes swept around his small audience, passing over Roland as airily as if he were barely visible. All the same, Roland knew he had been recognized.

Watching Quando, he felt he was watching two performances, one half hidden inside the other. Everyone was happy to applaud and wonder at the trickery of the first, but the other act, the hidden one, was something far stranger and more ironic. For suppose the magical acts that were being performed were not merely the clever tricks they seemed to be. Suppose the announcement of trickery was a sort of masking, intended to disguise the fact that something truly magical was taking place.

"And now my last trick," announced Quando. "You, sir! Yes, you at the back. Perhaps you could help me." And at last he was looking directly at Roland.

With a feeling of resignation Roland rose to his feet.

"We've met before, haven't we?" Quando asked, smiling as Roland walked to the stage. "Many years ago. I never forget a face. Now, you're not claustrophobic, are you? You're not frightened of being shut in? You're not frightened of . . . of *blackness*?"

"No way," said Roland. "I enjoy it." He was pleased at the lightness of his tone.

"Oh, sir!" cried Quando lightly. "What an admission. Mind you, there are mysteries about this box here. There's more space inside than outside it." He looked past Roland at the audience. "You think I'm joking, don't you, but this box is a box of marvels." He hit the lid with his wand, tapped the base. "It's solid, you see. No secret panels—no hidden compartments. So, indulge me, sir. You don't mind lying down inside it, do you?"

"Glad to!" said Roland. There was an inevitability about the steps that now carried him toward Quando. Where were all his smart answers? And where was his power to turn and walk away? But did he really *want* to walk away? Perhaps he wanted to live through it all again and get a final power over whatever happened to him. Quando was busily unfolding a little blue stepladder at the side of the coffin.

"Just step into the box, sir. That's right. Comfortable, mmmm? Wriggle around. Make yourself at home. Now! I'm going to close the lid for a few brief moments."

Roland found, as he settled into the box, that any questions of wanting or not wanting to be shut into the coffin made no sense. He believed he had been working his way over years and years toward stepping into that box once more. Quando looked in at him, possibly smiling back at him. His back was to the audience, and only Roland could see the intense interest in his ginger eyes. Were they asking questions? Could be! Were they making promises? Perhaps! Issuing threats? Quite possibly. The lid closed, and he heard the click of the latch.

Blackness. Hardly surprising. But it wasn't the blackness of a closed box. Without quite meaning to, he had closed his eyes . . . closed them so tightly that it felt as if he had managed, from within himself, to tape them shut. It took an act of will to open them again, but when he did, he found himself back in that place he had dreamed of ever since he had hung there the first time, the place into which he had fitted so well. Once again his arms were held out to embrace the space out there—that dark, clear, endless space, dusted with suns. It was exactly as he remembered it. For the dream—the trick, the memory, whatever it was—was a true part of him . . . always had been . . . always would be. And those suns, along with the unseen planets he now knew to be circling them—well, he was a true part of them, too. No *more* than they were, yet certainly no *less.* Then, in infinite distance, a new point of light sprang to life, to flare and grow in brilliance as it came wheeling toward him. He watched its approach with tranquil pleasure, knowing it must be Jess Ferret—Jess Ferret, burning as she came, transformed from girl to star of power. She was moving at colossal speed. Her brilliance seemed to be part of her momentum. He could not move out of her way, nor did he want to, though it seemed they must crash into each other. Would they shatter into glittering dust, or melt together, blazing up and springing into new life as a single star?

But then Roland was flooded, once more, with the light of common day. He blinked. The face of a phantom clown came down toward his. Quando was offering him his hand, just as he had done in that dream—not that it really had been a dream. From now on he must admit to himself that it was a memory. But this time Roland was determined to manage on his own. He sat up and grinned at the audience. People were exclaiming and applauding even as they stood up, gathering their bags and parcels, anxious to make for home. Quando turned and bowed to them all, then turned back to Roland, but Roland was already stepping out of the coffin onto the blue stepladder and down to solid ground once more.

"Thank you very much," Quando was saying to the crowd. "You saw him—and then you didn't see him. He couldn't possibly have disappeared, could he, and yet he did. But life is always more remarkable than we think it is. And that is my last trick for the day. Thank you, sir," he went on, looking directly at Roland. Beyond him people—mainly mothers and children—were filing out of the tent, looking back over their shoulders, still smiling in wonder.

"What did they see?" asked Roland.

"Why, they saw you get into the box, and then when it was opened, they saw it was empty," said Quando. "You weren't there, were you?" He opened the box once more and looked into it. "Quite solid, you see!" He thumped its top and sides. "No revolving sections." He looked at Roland, his eyes small and intense enough to peer into a heart of stone. "You know, you have a remarkable talent—well, you *could* have a talent, I mean to say. It isn't quite there yet, is it? You haven't named it, or invited it in—if you get my meaning."

"I don't, though," said Roland. "Get your meaning, that is."

"Oh, well, you have a *possible* talent, perhaps a *remarkable* talent," said Quando. "Let's leave it at that."

"No! Hang about!" cried Roland. "A talent's *for* something. This talent I'm supposed to have—what's it *for*?"

"I'm not certain if it's ever going to be fulfilled," said Quando, answering a different question from the one Roland was asking him. "Talents like yours usually come to nothing. Which may be a good thing. They aren't always comfortable, talents. Often we're better off without them. We're often happier—much happier—if we give them away."

Then he turned and began to pack the things from his table into a suitcase.

"That's not a proper answer," cried Roland defiantly.

A Proper Answer

Quando turned to face him. Something shifted under the thick white paint, and suddenly his face was merely the face of a clown. The black cloak hanging around him no longer stirred with supernatural suggestion, but hung limply—exhausted cloth quite possibly in need of a wash.

"Look! Thanks for your cooperation," he said, smiling.

Under the paint his mouth seemed to curve up more on the right cheek than it did on the left. He must be smiling. White powder fell out of the creases of the smile. He looked right, then left. "I do hope the kindergarten has done well from this afternoon. As for you and me, let's sashay into the mall and have a drink of some kind. I suppose you're of an age to have a glass of wine with an old friend? My treat."

"What?" said Roland, looking around the tent, then over at the coffin. "Leave all your stuff here?" Now, as the little fair continued to dismantle itself, Quando's basket of boxes, bright globes, puppets, cards, and deceiving shawls already looked half lost and pathetic. Who could believe any sort of magic beyond the familiar tricks of a conjurer had ever resided in them?

"No, no. I'll drive my van down here and put everything neatly in the back," said Quando. "It won't take me long." He turned away, then turned back again. "Don't disappear on me," he said a little archly.

Roland waited on the bank, watching the last of the organizers—all women—stalking to and fro in the late-afternoon light. Across the river Jess's house crouched behind other houses, thrusting the long drive between its neat hedges toward him like an extended tongue. *Yah! Yah! Yah!* that house was saying. *You thought you'd creep up on me again, didn't you? But you walked straight into a trap. Yah!*

And the haunting, detailed dream of his childhood was shifting around in his head, coming to bits, then putting itself together again.

Careful, said his warning voice. *Careful!*

But I have to know, he argued silently. *I mean, who the hell* is *this Quando?* He began to list the reasons why he should take an interest. *I've remembered him as a dream all these years, but now I know he* wasn't *a dream. And I know he was the one standing behind me at the tennis court the other day. "Fabuloso." He said it aloud. Same voice, anyway. And there's someone else he reminds me of, though I can't think who. Suddenly, he's gone from being nowhere to being everywhere. Quando can't be his real name, so who is he? And what does he want? Because I know he wants something.*

A green van was angling itself into a place that seemed too small to hold it, but the driver obviously knew just what he and his van could do. QUANDO THE MAGICIAN, proclaimed faded letters painted on its side, scarlet on green. Roland watched as the nightmare dream of his childhood dissolved, becoming part of a roughly conforming, everyday life in which things had to be folded, stored, and packed away. Quando, minus his black crown but with his face still painted white, his braids still swinging, his cloak still swishing, strolled toward Roland across the Riverlaw Reserve.

"Can I give you a hand?" Roland asked, and found himself, a few minutes later, wheeling the coffin up the small slope and helping to slide it into the back of the van . . . a van that was immaculately clean inside. He watched Quando wind up the colored cords, put the silver pegs in a box, and collapse the tent, which seemed to fall into folds with an eerie accuracy and ease. Following directions, Roland helped to fold the tent into the back of the green van, after which Quando arranged his various boxes with a finicky, fluttering care, almost as if he were arranging flowers.

"A little time and trouble now makes such a difference later on," he lisped, giving his masked smile once more. "Ah! Now I'll just lock the door, and we'll be off and away!"

Careful! said Roland's inner voice.

Quando locked the back of the van and left it parked on the edge of the green strip, ignoring a sign that declared all parking was limited to fifteen minutes.

"It's late," he said, waving a hand at the notice as he walked past it. "They won't be prowling around here at this time of day."

He walked a little ahead of Roland, almost as if he owned the reserve and were showing it off.

"Unexpected little place, isn't it? Tucked away here like a city secret," he said. "Now, if I remember correctly, there's a way through to the street somewhere along here. Ah, yes!" He turned abruptly into the alley, weaving his way skillfully between the garbage bags, which were once more bulging beyond their doorsteps.

Light and bustle welcomed them onto the main road, and Roland caught himself sighing with relief. He was back in real life again. The Riverlaw Reserve, that unreliable country, its boundaries (in spite of any NO EXIT signs) shifty and unresolved, was behind him.

"Admit it! We *have* met before, haven't we?" Quando insisted as they approached the arched doorway of the mall.

"At the tennis match the other day," said Roland. "We were watching the same game."

"Yes, but before then," Quando persisted. "Oh, ages ago! When you were the merest infant at the time!"

"Might have, I suppose," said Roland, lying yet again. "I don't remember, though."

Just beyond the arch that announced the mall, the café glittered blue and silver. Obediently following Quando, Roland entered the café and sat down next to the window at a table Quando had chosen. The eclipsing shadows of outside passers-by swept again and again over the shining surface in front of him. Quando went to the counter and returned with a small tray, on which stood a bottle of white wine and two glasses.

He's just trying to flatter you, said the voice in his head. *He wants something from you.*

I already know *that!* Roland told himself, irritated by his own well-meaning advice. *But, no sweat! Because I'm going to find out something from him.*

And he knows it! And he knows it! said the voice, considerably more clamorous than usual.

"It's wonderful to get to the end of a day," said Quando. He relaxed back into the café chair in a luxurious, sagging fashion, ignoring the people who were looking over at him, no doubt intrigued by the blank white oval looking out from between the black braids. "I mean, it's what I've chosen. It's what I want. But people don't realize just how tiring it can be to be a magician." As he looked directly at Roland his ginger-colored eyes seemed to contract momentarily into slits. Roland had seen this effect before in other eyes. He recognized it with a sort of prickling alarm, though this time he did not have that feeling of looking along a tear-shaped tunnel into infinite space. What he *seemed* to glimpse was a savage and all-devouring desire grimacing out at him. It was there for only a moment, jaws wide, and then he was meeting a bland gaze once more.

"We *have* met, you know," Quando insisted once more. "A long time ago, when I was a much younger magician . . . I was putting on one of my acts . . . early days for me. Actually, if I remember correctly, I asked your *father* to climb into my wonder box so that he could be part of a little disappearing act for the delectation of my public—by the way, *delectation* means 'pleasure.' . . ."

"Yeah, I know that," said Roland lightly, pleased that his voice should be so firm yet mild. "I do understand a few unusual words."

"Congratulations, then," Quando said. "And I'm sorry if I sounded patronizing. In these days of liberal education one never knows just how much a young person fails to learn. What I was trying to tell you is that your father must have been a shy man, because he made you his sacrifice, as it were. He stepped back and pushed you forward, and a little later you disappeared so beautifully—oh, and reappeared, *of course.* You were only a very small boy at the time, but don't you remember it at all? Surely you must."

"I don't think so," said Roland. "Actually, I don't even remember my father all that well. He took off ages ago."

"You look like him," said Quando. "Indeed, that's probably how I came to recognize you—because you look so much like your father, whom I seem to recall vividly for some reason. I'll never forget him stepping back but pushing his child forward, as I said, like a sort of sacrifice. What cowards grown men can be."

"If I was such a little kid," said Roland, "I probably wouldn't remember."

He sipped the wine in what he hoped was a sophisticated fashion. Quando leaned forward.

"When you were in my wonder box did you *see* anything?" he asked. His voice was light and laughing, as if they were joking with each other, yet something lurking under this open tone gave the question an unexpected intensity.

"Well, it was dark, of course," said Roland. "Really dark! And something moved. I heard it. I mean, you must know what it's like. Or haven't you tried it yourself?" His question came out as more of an open challenge than he had intended.

Quando sat back.

"Well, I have tried it," he admitted, "but every now and then," he went on, speaking with particular care, "I find myself working with someone who—well, how can I explain this most accurately? I find myself working with someone who lies in my wonder box and perceives something more than mere darkness under a closed lid."

Take care! screamed the inner voice with particular urgency. But Roland had already screwed up his face, assuming the expression of someone who did not have the faintest idea what Quando was talking about.

"What sort of thing?" he asked. "How could you see more than darkness when someone shuts you in a box?"

"Occasionally I do find a person who can see . . . who sees . . ." Quando suddenly seemed unsure of himself. "Who sees visions," he said at last.

Roland laughed. "Are you for real?" he cried.

"Yes," said Quando, sounding defensive. "I am 'for real,' as you put it. I'm asking a serious question."

"I don't see visions," Roland declared robustly. "I'm not into that stuff."

Quando turned the wine bottle toward himself, apparently reading the label, but Roland, who was putting on a performance of his own, found it easy to recognize another person's acting. When Quando looked up at Roland once more, it was with a glance so sharp it was rather, Roland thought, like being stabbed.

"You don't have to be afraid to admit any strangeness to me," he said softly. "I can read it in you. I know it's there."

"You know more than I do, then," cried Roland with an indignation that was almost genuine. "There isn't any strangeness in me that I know of."

Then both he and Quando sat back, and both drank wine, rather as if they were each other's reflection, though Quando drank more, and rather more quickly, than Roland. Silence fell between them. It was almost as if they had nothing left to say to each other.

Attack! commanded the voice in Roland's mind.

"So, are you trying to make out I'm gay or something?" he demanded rather aggressively. "Is that what you're getting at when you talk about strangeness?"

"No, no, nothing like that," said Quando quickly and placatingly. "No! But every now and then I do meet people who seem to me to have . . . an extra sense, let's say . . . people who might actually be able to move the world with a secret power that is all their own."

"Are you talking about *magic*?" Roland asked, injecting strong incredulity into his voice.

"I suppose that *is* one of the words—a common word, a totally inadequate one for what I am talking about," Quando replied.

"And you reckon you're magical?" asked Roland. There was a long silence.

"To some extent," said Quando at last. "That's why I'm able to recognize it in others."

"Hey! Whoa! Chill out!" cried Roland, overdoing things. "I mean, for one thing, you must have taken years to learn those tricks you do, so you must *know* that they're tricks. Because just supposing you do have real magical power, why are you poncing around in a wig, pulling colored scarves out of empty boxes in the Riverlaw Reserve? Why aren't you the king of the world or something like that?"

Laughing a little, Quando drank his wine. It was impossible to tell, under all that white paint, how he was really reacting to Roland's question.

"Oh, I'm working my way toward king of the world," he said at last. "Conjuring isn't all I do. I do have another job—quite a demanding one. But if I have made some sort of mistake where you are concerned . . ." He broke off, and fine white powder sifted down onto the table below him and even into his glass. Roland thought he might be frowning inside his mask. "But I'm *not* mistaken," Quando declared softly. "It is just that you don't fully recognize your own nature—your own ability—as yet. And then, perhaps, you don't want to live a life that has any incalculable element in it," he went on. "Be honest! You must already know I am more than a mere conjurer." He drained his glass and then refilled it. "Look! I dabble in hypnosis. I wonder if you would let me . . . if you would agree to—"

"No way!" cried Roland, leaping to his feet. Quando stood up abruptly too.

"That's all right! Quite all right," he said in a low voice, fluttering his left hand as he spoke. The woman behind the counter stared at them. "That's fine. Forget it. Forget it all for now."

"I have to get home, anyway," Roland said, and drained his own glass in a way he hoped looked polished and confident. "Thanks for the drink," he added. "Perhaps we'll meet again in another ten years or whatever."

At the door he turned to smile or wave or say good-bye in some way and saw Quando watching him go. Though it was impossible to read his expression, Roland could feel a wave of fury surging toward him. But Roland refused to recognize it. Waving and nodding, he walked out of the café. Then, once outside and out of sight, he ran for his mother's car.

Great! You did well, said the voice in his head, but Roland already knew this. He did not bother to reply.

All the same, just what is *going on?* he asked himself later, lying in bed, getting ready to sleep. *And I don't just mean* what *is going on. It's more a matter of how many things are going on, and whether they fit together. I've got to work them out and put them in order. They feel as if they must be connected. But how can they be? First there was Mr. Hudson blackmailing me . . . wanting me to cuddle up to Jess Ferret.* His attempt at putting the events of the last few days in some sort of connected order was interrupted by a yawn. He sighed impatiently, then yawned again, falling asleep in the very act of putting things in order, for though he was alarmed by the tangle, he was also exhausted by it.

PUTTING THINGS IN ORDER

Mind you, old Hudson trying to blackmail me was not *the first thing,* he was telling himself as he woke in the morning, just as if six hours of sleep hadn't interrupted his thinking for a moment. Then he paused, wondering exactly what he had been telling himself as he slept. *Come on! Get it straight!* he thought, propping himself up against the pillows, and frowning and blinking. *There was my little bit of shoplifting. Right! That was the* first *thing.* The supermarket aisle came vividly back into his mind. Yes. He could see himself there—Roland Fairfield, man of the Fairfield family, his mother's great white hope, pushing groceries in a supermarket shopping cart. *Yes, again!* There he was, holding the red notebook and pretending to assess its suitability for some entirely fictional purpose. There were the two women by the card display, passing cards from one to the other, laughing as they did so, and there was the man in the black coat, slightly turned away from him and studying a length of wrapping paper. Roland's eyes sprang open. *Oh, God! Yes! The man in the black coat! Quando!*

Fully awake now, he found himself recalling how Mr. Hudson had walked past him in the school yard almost a week ago, waving to someone near the bike shed. He remembered a crowd of Crichton kids collecting their bikes, remembered Tom on duty, and remembered, there among the waiting mothers, a man in a black coat. His gaze swung toward the bottom drawer of his desk. Roland frowned and bit his lip. That day in the supermarket someone had been telling him what to do, and without realizing that he was under orders, he had done it. The original gift he had accepted from Quando all those years ago had established a point of entry—one that Quando had been able to use. And it must have been Quando who had supplied the objects, which in due course Mr. Hudson had lined up on the desk in front of him; it must have been Quando who had wanted to know what was going on in Jess Ferret's house and just who was at home there.

There was a thump on a door farther down the hall.

"Come on, you kids! Get up! Get going!" Roland's mother

usually began the day by yelling at Danny and Martin. She thumped on his door in turn.

"Roley! Wake up! It's a school day and I need the car, so you'll just have to bike."

"I'm up!" he lied, and heard her shouting at Martin and Danny once more, just to make sure. They were never as responsible as he was when it came to getting ready for breakfast and school.

First, I shoplifted three pens, a pie, and a notebook, Roland thought as he dressed for the day ahead. *Dumb move! Mind you, I mightn't have been totally responsible, because there was Quando—well, now I know it was Quando—just down the aisle. And the things I stole were a sort of parallel to the things he gave me in my dream—not that it* was *a dream. Second, Mr. Hudson knew about my shoplifting, which could be because Quando* told *him, which means they must know each other, or perhaps Quando has some power over him, too. And Mr. Hudson began blackmailing me. . . .* Roland felt he was using the term with even more accuracy than when he had first used it almost a week ago. *I was to cozy up to Jess Ferret. And there are connections there, too, because who pops up in the Riverlaw Reserve, right opposite Jess's house? Quando again! Mr. Everywhere All at Once! QED! Quando Enters Disguised. Anyhow, I did try to move in on Jess. I went to her house. Because, third, Jess is a different proposition in her house from what she is at school. Well, fair enough! Most of us are. But her house is weird, and not just word-weird—I mean her house is truly weird . . .* accurately *weird. And there's no sign of any parents. And she doesn't like being asked about them, though it's them that Mr. Hudson really wants to know about—well, about her mother, anyway. It's her mother he mostly asks about, which might mean it's her mother Quando is interested in. But not having any parents in residence is not the really weird thing about Jess's house. The thing is it's frozen—utterly unchanging frozen. Frozen in time, I suppose. Which is a lot of rubbish, and yet it's true. And I* know *it. I don't believe in ghosts, but there was something pretty* close *to a ghost at the top of the stairs. . . .*

"Breakfast!" shouted his mother. "Get a move on!"

"I'll eat his," offered Danny.

Later in the day, sitting with the gang under the library windows and staring across the school yard at Jess, Roland found he was still trying to put things into useful order.

It's all linked, he was thinking, *but how can it be linked? That Quando dream that's turned out to be real, all* that *began years ago, ages before I knew Jess or Mr. Hudson. And then there's the* breathing*! I don't seem to be able to push it back—not in the way I used to. Listen to it now.* And against the advice of his inner voice he did listen, shaking his head slowly as he did so.

Divide, divide! the breathing was telling him—or perhaps it was really talking to itself, and he was accidentally listening. *Multiply . . . divide . . . cleave, cleave, cleave . . .*

Forget all that, his inner voice was trying to command him. *Flow, flow, embrace, cleave, enfold, enfold, enfold . . .*

"Hey, wake up, man," said a voice, Stephen's voice. Startled, Roland looked around to find his friends staring at him and realized they had been expecting him to make some comment about something—to answer a question, maybe—but he had been caught up in that overpowering inner sound. Even in the second or two in which he had been listening to it, it had become more urgent and insistent than any of the voices around him.

"He's away with the la-las," cried Chris, and her expression was not altogether kind. Roland looked at her placatingly, but the truth was, when it came to women, Jess Ferret was dominating his thoughts right then. *If I go to her place tonight,* he thought, *if I make her talk about herself, she might tell me something that would explain all this. I've got to understand what's going on. Nothing will work well for me until I do. Okay! I'll pin Jess down. I'll ferret around her until she tells me everything she knows. That's part of the fifth point. So I'll shoot home after school, work like mad on my assignments, and then I'll drop in on Jess and make her talk her head off.*

THE THIRD TIME

Late that afternoon Roland walked onto the green bank of the Riverlaw Reserve for the third time. The grass was trodden flat—a little bruised. The comings and goings of the Riverlaw Kindergarten fair had left their mark. Passing the place where Quando's tent had been raised the previous day, Roland caught himself turning his head away and forced himself to look squarely back again. He could make out the place where the coffin must have stood. Why, he wondered, did he still think of it as a coffin, when Quando had called it, rather more accurately, a wonder box? Then, raising his eyes, he stared across the river to the calm, enigmatic frontage of Jess Ferret's tall house, with its closed green door.

"'Childe Roland to the dark tower came,'" he muttered.

Crossing the footbridge and then the road beyond, he approached Jess's front door with trepidation, but with other feelings too, for this time he was *choosing* to call on Jess for his own reasons, and not simply because of Mr. Hudson's blackmail. This time he *wanted* to see her, because she had become part of a puzzle he was determined to solve.

All day he had felt himself laced through with the things Quando had said to him. Was it really some unnamed talent that had enabled him to hang among the stars? And did he share it with Jess Ferret, who had spun toward him like a wheel of fire? Did he share it with Quando? Perhaps not, for Quando had really wanted to know just what Roland had experienced once that coffin lid closed over him. Twice now he had leaned eagerly toward Roland, longing to be told. Anyhow, here he was, Childe Roland, walking up to Jess's house, determined that, somehow or other, he would make her tell him all the things that Quando must not know. He already knew that whenever Jess stepped in through her green front door, she stepped into strangeness—after all, he had already stepped into it himself. Now he would try to work out exactly what was going on. Understanding it all seemed to be the only way in which he could fight his way back to being the man he had been last Friday morning.

As he approached it he felt Jess's door giving off mystery like leftover summer heat, felt its inner strangeness come beating toward him. The day at school, time spent working on his assignments, twitched a little in his head and then died on him. Chris's irritation with him, along with home life, school life, and Mr. Hudson's questioning eyebrows, all the day's connections fell away from him like dead ash. Only that door was real.

It turned out that door was open—just a little open. Standing next to it, he was able to see the thread of darkness between the door's edge and its frame. Roland raised his hand to knock, then changed his mind and pushed instead.

"Hello!" he called into the widening slot of shadow. "Jess! Are you there? Is anyone home?"

There was no reply.

"It's me!" he called. "Roley Fairfield! Is anyone home?"

Silence.

"Is anyone home?" he called more loudly, and wondered what he would say if Jess's mother actually appeared, filled with ordinary adult irritation at an unexpected invasion. He began working out what excuses he would give, only to find he was completely certain that there would be no one at home—well, no one except Jess. The house felt . . . not empty, but certainly empty of anything as homely as parents.

"Hey, Jess!" he called again, peering through the widening gap as he looked nervously for any change of light. There was still no reply. Two steps and he was through that door, leaving it slightly open behind him, just as he had found it.

The hall was not just shadowy, but filled with deep twilight. Apart from the altered light it seemed not just more or less the same as it had been last Saturday evening, but *exactly* the same. He *knew* that the folds in the coats hanging on their hooks, the alignment of the shoes and boots below them, were *precisely* as they had been last Saturday, that the threads fringing the strip of carpet were spread identically in last Saturday's pattern, unmoved by any of the exits or entrances that must have taken place since he first stepped through the green door. But then, in Jess's house everything was fixed forever, caught in a particular moment of time from which there was neither advance nor retreat. Somehow Jess's hands had managed to slide backward and forward over the dust on the handrail of the stairs without disturbing it; her feet would have trodden those fringes of the carpet without altering their pale scribble against the dark wood below. Slowly, almost unwillingly, Roland raised his eyes to look up the stairs. *There won't be anyone there,* he told himself. But there at the top he saw—he definitely saw, in spite of the soft gloom of the landing—someone looking down at him.

He knew he would remember forever each detail of the face looking back at his. Even though they were separated by the height of the stairs and the shadows of that late-autumn afternoon, he had seen clearly. He would remember not its expression, for it wore no expression he could recognize, but the silhouette of its springing hair and the shape of its eyes, dark against pale skin. Above all else, he would remember it as unearthly, for it was sharing the space of the hall and landing with him through some unnatural accident. It should have belonged—*would* have belonged, if Jess's house had been part of the acceptable world—to another sort of space entirely. When Jess smiled, sending her smiles inward as well as out, it was to a hidden presence very like this that she was directing them. Now, due to some terrible error, it had become visible in the outside world, and he was the one who had been chosen to see it.

As he looked up Roland found he was willing it to show itself more clearly, was willing it to speak to him or to reveal itself in some way. This it did by stepping forward. He had seen it before, of course—well, he had half seen it over Jess's shoulder as he said good-bye at the end of his first visit—but this time there was no Jess to thrust herself in front of him and hurry him out through the front door. The creature up there, whatever it was, could stare down at him, and he could stare back at it, without interruption.

The face looking down at him was beautiful—but beautiful in such a curious way that calling it beautiful did not seem like praise. Black hair tangled around its high cheekbones. Its full lips were a little parted in an arrested, feral eagerness that reminded Roland of the Medusa on the green door. Though he could not see the color of its eyes, he felt sure they would be blue and sharply defined with black lashes. And just as he began to feel it might be male, that it might even be old, he also felt utterly certain that both sex and age were irrelevant to the creature that seemed to be looking down at him.

"Hi!" he said, and his voice came out as a breathy whine. ("Jess?" he almost asked it.)

There was no reply. The black-haired creature gave no sign of having heard anything, but stepped sideways and then began to come, slowly, down the stairs toward him.

"Is Jess here?" he asked yet again, ashamed of the fear that began to fill him, yet determined not to retreat. "Jess! Is that *you*?" For he did wonder if it might be Jess transformed. His fear grew stronger at the creature's approach but was still not strong enough to dislodge his fascination. He had the impression that its outline wavered midstep, that it blurred and fluctuated in some way, but if this was so, it rapidly became fixed once more and continued its descent. "All right, I'll go . . . I'll go," said Roland, panting a little as he surrendered. "Tell her I . . ." But now the creature began to move rapidly, leaving the stairs and staring *at* him and *through* him as if it wasn't sure that *he* really existed. "Tell her . . . ," he shouted, dropping his bike helmet and flinging up his hands in both surrender and defense, as the creature came rushing toward him. It was right before him. It was *on* him—and then the whole world vanished.

SOMETHING WORSE THAN FEAR

Roland opened his eyes. Lying there on the floor, close to the foot of the staircase, he believed for a moment that he had been pressed flat, had become a museum specimen to be pinned up on Jess Ferret's wall. The whole world had been reduced to a frame. Gasping and blinking, he took a deep breath, staring up at the high ceiling of the Ferret hall, forcing depth back into everything, but at the mercy, it seemed, of the congregation of shadows crowding above him. A draft from the door (still slightly open) ruffled through his hair and stroked his sweating scalp. What had happened to him? Roland moved an arm, then bent his knees. There he was—no, *here* he was—flooded with hazy bewilderment, with huge fear lurking beyond the haze, but completely himself again. And was what felt like fear actually something *worse* than fear? After all, fear could be mastered, couldn't it? Or at any rate it could be lived through. People came out on the other side of fear. But there was no other side to what Roland was experiencing.

Alteration. He had been altered. Still lying on the floor, he turned his head and looked up toward the landing. It was quite empty. There was no sign of the creature that had come rushing toward him, to pass—yes—to pass right through him. To *live* in him. For a fraction of time he had been *inhabited.* Patterns that were part of the creature had sprung into urgent life inside *his* head; connections had been made—were still being made. He could feel something being pieced together, and some of the pieces being used were parts of himself. "I don't understand," he said aloud. But then understanding—normal understanding—seemed irrelevant. The creature, whatever it was, had become part of him for a moment of time. It had chosen (if anything as rational as choice was a possibility for a presence beyond all reason) to fuse itself into him, melting through muscle and bone, through cell to nucleus of cell and beyond. And though it was gone (he had no idea where), whatever it was—whatever it had been—would always be part of him from now on. Lying there on the floor in Jess Ferret's hall, he knew he was not the self that he had been ten minutes earlier, and that he would never be that original self ever again. Knowledge of the change horrified him.

There were steps on the other side of the green door; it was flung wide. Jess's voice cried out from somewhere above and behind him.

"Oh, *damn*!" she exclaimed. "Damn! Damn! Damn! What are *you* doing here?"

Roland sat up slowly.

"Are your parents home?" he asked, sounding so stupid he scarcely recognized himself. He certainly knew that the creature that had walked through him was not—could never be—anybody's parent.

"It's no business of yours," Jess cried frantically. She had an empty bowl in her hand, and she shook it at him as if at any moment she might hit him with it. "I keep telling you, I like to be alone."

"But you're not alone," he said.

"Get out!" she shouted. "Get out!"

In her own way she was transformed once more—transformed with rage and with more than rage. She had stopped pretending to be someone that she wasn't, as he now understood she did every day at school. There was nothing of that slightly dull, dogged Weaselly-Ferret presence. Her hair stood out around her face like tongues of black fire; her lips were parted as if she were about to pronounce a spell. Just for a moment Roland thought she might charge into him and then out the other side like the invading creature she so resembled. However, Jess was not a creature. Her fury was a human fury.

"It . . . it looked like you," he stammered, sounding stupid in his confusion. "Well, not quite like you. It was—"

"That way!" she cried again, shaking the bowl toward the door. "Out!"

"You shouldn't have left it open," he said. "I just . . ."

But now Jess was beyond words. She simply shook the bowl at him. Roland heaved himself onto his knees, then rose to his feet and stumbled for the door.

As he stepped out into the evening a wave—a wave of sound, a wave of something he was forced to call sound, as there was no other name to call it by, a wave of *something*—came rushing to meet him, curving over him, curving over and over him, never quite breaking, yet holding him in its field. That breathing he had recently grown to know so well—that same breathing became unimaginably huge, filled the city, filled the world, filled the universe. It beat up at him from the earth, smashed down on him from the sky. It burst at him from hedges and willows and from the water in front of him, moving so smoothly that it seemed to be standing still. Transfixed, Roland stood on the footpath outside Jess Ferret's house, knowing this irresistible invasion to be part of his continuing alteration. The few people strolling in the Riverlaw Reserve would be unaware of it. The giant breathing of the world was being heard by him, and by him alone. Then, through it all, he heard yet another sound—the clap and click of the green door closing and locking behind him.

Roland did not turn. He stood there, entirely possessed by the sigh of an immense sea, but knowing all the time that in ordinary life—the life he had been living only a few days earlier—the sea was far away, on the other side of the city hills.

On a Riverside Bench

He walked slowly back across the footbridge but found he could not bring himself to go home straightaway. Instead he sank down onto one of the seats in the reserve and sat there, unnaturally still, looking out across the river toward Jess's house. He felt for his bike helmet in a distracted fashion, even though he already knew he had left it in the hall behind that green door and that he did not have the will to reclaim it right then.

"Changed! I've been changed," he muttered to himself, just to hear what this idea sounded like in the outer world, studying first the backs of his hands and then, rather more closely, his palms, in case he might see an altered fortune scribbled there. "Changing! I'm changing!" Inside or out, he knew it was true. What he could not understand was just how he was changing. He was certain he would be recognizable. When he arrived home, none of his family would stare at him, alarmed to find a stranger coming boldly through their door. Any rearrangement that might be taking place would not be visible. An inky mark on his right-hand forefinger intrigued him; an ordinary, grubby life was patiently waiting for him to start living it once again.

Soon, he promised it silently. Something had pushed him out of that life, and now his job was to work his way back into it once more. Raising his head, he looked around him.

Lights were on. People strolling in the reserve were looking out at the river and at the trailing willows, backs turned to the loading bays on the other side of the road. Some people were within speaking distance, but all those strolling around seemed to exist in a different state from his own. Roland felt he was either the only real person in a world of ghosts or, perhaps, the only ghost in a world of real people. After watching the passersby vaguely for a minute or two, he began to stretch, straightening his shoulders as if to remind himself just how he was fitted together. "The head bone's connected to the neck bone," he mumbled. The really peculiar thing was that he was already beginning to feel *truer* being a possible ghost than he had felt earlier in the day as the man of the family or as a successful Crichton Academy prefect. He looked at his watch. Twenty minutes! Only twenty minutes ago he had been someone—no! some*thing*—different.

The creature had not just faced him. It had walked through him. It hadn't asked him a riddle, hadn't requested an answer or a gift, as creatures in fairy tales were supposed to do. It had just walked though him. He had felt—what *had* he felt? Something like a sting of cold, except that it hadn't been cold. Something like an electric shock, except that he hadn't been plugged into any current. And now here he was, wave after wave of sensation rushing toward him, rearing but never quite toppling. He could hear the universe breathing. He was sitting still on the bench in the Riverlaw Reserve, yet at the same time, he was in continual motion. And every single thing in the world out there, every single solitary thing, no matter how big, no matter how small, was somehow *singing* at him. It was all too much. Much too much!

He closed his eyes and counted to ten, but the song refused to retreat. He opened first one eye and then the other. Every surface, each object, immediately became more than he could understand or bear to think about. It was as if he must, from this moment forward, be constantly aware of elements grappling one another in the great multiple embraces that held things together. Each statement of position and each intricate linkage sang at him. Holding up his hand once more, Roland looked experimentally at his fingers, black against the light reflecting from the stream below. There they were, ten of them, covered in skin that was always renewing itself, shedding old cells, building up new—and he seemed to be able to trace the blood and bone that lay beneath it. It was quite different from merely reading about blood and skin in a biology text, or learning about them by studying diagrams for an exam. This is what he *was*: a melting, changing creature, going up and out, appearing and disappearing, in a perpetually constant-inconstant world.

"And how do you feel tonight?" asked a voice.

Roland lowered his hand and looked sideways, already knowing whom he was going to see. That slight lisp was unmistakable by now. Quando the Magician was looming over him, his face naked of any white paint but still difficult to make out properly, for he was standing with his back to the streetlights, and the brim of his black hat was casting a deep shadow over the face below it. All the same, Roland knew that Quando was looking at him with an excited intensity.

"I happened to be wandering around here about half an

hour ago and I felt a disturbance in the Force," Quando said, and laughed a little—more of a giggle than a true laugh. "Don't you think it is time we talked to each other properly? Because I can feel your distress. And I can help you. I can really help you. I can set you free of the weight of it. Lift the burden."

Roland stared at him. "Why are you spying on Jess Ferret?" he asked.

Quando stepped back. "I don't know what you're talking about, actually," he said.

"Well, leave me alone!" Roland cried, astonished by the violence in his own voice. The words rushed out of him. "Get stuffed—*actually! Actually,* bite your bum—if you can bend back that far!" He leaped to his feet. "*Actually!*" he added by way of a full stop.

"Oh, what suggestions!" said Quando lightly. "Sit down again. Let's talk."

But Roland was pushing past Quando, first stumbling, then running, longing at last for his own house, and his own room, with the door firmly shut behind him. He wove his way down the alley, falling once but picking himself up again and running on, ignoring his outraged elbows and knees. Then he was out on the main road once more—the blessed main road, where people weren't drifting spirits and where he no longer felt as if he were a different form of existence. Unlocking his bicycle and then riding off on it required nothing but simple common sense. A few minutes of careful pedaling carried him not only toward his home, but slowly back into the familiar, rational world again. It was true that, as he shot forward, the great breathing sound that was not a sound moved with him, but so did the sound of the city's traffic.

"Yay!" shouted Roland, letting go and flinging both arms into the air, loving and embracing the roar of approaching cars, which seemed to ask nothing of him except simple avoidance. All he had to do was to keep from toppling himself under their wheels. Altered and still altering, illegally helmetless but feeling in charge of himself once more, Roland biked home in perfect safety.

Family Histories

"Trickery!" Roland said aloud, and woke abruptly into the familiar dark of his bedroom. He was lying on his bed not in it, wrapped around in the stifling, stale, crumpled feeling that comes from sleeping half the night away in clothes of the day before. Though he had been sleeping, he did not feel refreshed, but weary and disreputable, and he picked himself up from his bed as if he were climbing out of a gutter. As he did this he was immediately aware of two things. One was that he was still the vortex of a breathing storm, the other was that he had not finished his school assignments, which he must do. Even if the stolen goods in his desk drawer began piping reproachful songs at him, even if Jess Ferret flew in at the skylight to hover and shout like an angel of vengeance, he must complete those assignments. The figures on the face of his alarm clock shone in the darkness like a circle of little ghosts. It was after half past twelve.

Yawning and shaking his head, Roland sat on the edge of his bed pulling himself together. Feet? Yes! Legs? Yes! Hands and arms? Right! Head? Must be there! He clasped it, turned it right, then left, half expecting his broken thoughts to rattle around in it. Yes! Head in place. That just had to be enough to go on with. Wearily he picked himself up and made for the door. If anyone needed something to drink, he did. His throat was dry to the point of crackling. Believing he must be the only person awake in the silent house, he walked down the hall planning to weave his way through the sitting room and into the kitchen beyond it, well able to find his way without turning on any lights. Then, as he opened the sitting-room door, shivering, he heard from somewhere beyond it a long sigh, which he immediately recognized. It was not a part of any ghostly sound, however. It was simply that the heater had been left on.

There was a startled movement in the chair beside the heater. Light sprang from the little lamp on the fireside table. Roland found he was confronting his mother, who began pulling herself upright in her chair, blinking and yawning at him. Earlier in the evening she must have been experimenting with new hairstyles. At any rate, she was wearing her hair in a short braid, very much as Chris wore hers.

"Hi, Mum," he said quickly. "Cup of tea? I certainly need one."

"Oh, dear, you shouldn't be working so late," his mother said, and yawned again. "I must have nodded off."

"You and me both!" said Roland, swinging sideways into the kitchen but leaving the sliding door open so that they could talk to each other if they wished to. He turned on the light and immediately felt himself becoming an actor on a small, bright stage, performing for an audience of one.

"It must be midnight," said his mother vaguely.

"Yeah, it's half past glass-slipper time," agreed Roland. "But I can do midnight easily."

"You're such a good boy," said his mother, peering fondly toward the lit kitchen.

"Well, for God's sake, don't spread it around," Roland replied, shaking old, soggy tea bags from the belly of the teapot and finding it, as ever, hard to cope with open praise from his mother. "You'll ruin my reputation."

"Funny, isn't it?" Mrs. Fairfield said, still sounding sleepy. "Why do kids of your age just hate the thought of being *good*?" Then she spoke his name in rather a different voice. "Roland!"

Roland, who had been moving around the lit cell of their small kitchen, paused to peer apprehensively back into the dim sitting room. From here, with her back to the little lamp, his mother was a featureless black shape. Only her edges were shining.

"What?" he asked cautiously. Mrs. Fairfield laughed as she leaned forward and turned off the lamp at her elbow.

"You don't need to sound so scared," she said rather derisively. "I just wanted to say your name so that I could hear what it sounded like all over again. And I'm going to tell you what a good kid you are whether you like it or not. Don't think I don't notice just because I don't mention it."

"Oh, Mum!" Roland exclaimed impatiently.

"I know! I know!" she said, still laughing, but now with a sort of sadness in her voice. "It's hard to take a mother's compliments."

Which was true. Though he was filled with pleasure to think he was helping her to be happy, he did not want her *telling* him about it.

"There's no need to say anything," he said. "Just forget it and let things flow on." But Mrs. Fairfield was not to be diverted.

"When I listen to other mums talk, I realize how lucky I am," she said. Roland grimaced as he pulled the tea cozy over the teapot, half thinking he should put it over his own head to make himself safely faceless. "You look like your old man, but, mind you, you're already twice the man he was. He was always making out he was so tough, but deep down he was—I don't know—*unfinished,* I suppose. Afraid of life. Oh, and afraid of his mother as well. She was a real tartar. You're lucky having a mother like me."

"Mum, forget it!" Roland said again. "Let's forget it. Forget Dad, too. He's forgotten us."

"There you are," said his mother, sounding much less sleepy. "Just then you looked exactly the way he used to look in his good moments."

"I've always looked like him," Roland replied. "Or that's what people say."

"Yes," she agreed, "but there were times when he had—I don't know—a special look. A sort of brightness. It came and went. And just now you sort of flared up in the way he used to."

"I'll probably slump back into being my old dull self at any second," said Roland. He made the tea while the heater hissed expressionlessly.

"Cup or mug?" Roland asked at last. "Say a mug, because I've already poured it."

"Mug," said his mother obediently. "And then come and sit down for a moment. We don't get a chance to enjoy much silence, what with the younger kids always around. Everything is always in such an uproar. And it'll be good for you to get a break from all your work."

"I've had a break," Roland said quickly. "I told you. I went to sleep. I've got stuff to finish."

"Ten minutes won't hurt you," she replied easily. "Come on! Do what you're told."

Roland carried in two mugs of tea, setting one down at his mother's end of the hearth, then slumping down in the chair opposite hers.

"You're getting on so well," she said, and then added hastily, "not that I'm going to run on about it, but I'm entitled to do a bit of quiet trumpeting when there's no one else to hear—"

But Roland now found there was something he wanted to ask his mother. "Mum," he interrupted her, "do you remember Dad taking me to see a magician back when I was small—about four years old, I suppose? I seem to have some picture of it in my mind from way back. Did he ever say anything about it to you?"

His mother, wrapped in her shadows, sat quietly, no doubt sifting her own memories.

"He did take you out on the weekend sometimes," she replied rather uncertainly. "He really loved you, you know. That's why I still can't . . . but never mind that. When it comes to magicians, it might be Dad's dad you're remembering. Now, he really, truly *was* a magician."

"Grandad Fairfield? A magician?" exclaimed Roland. He struggled to remember his father's father. The image of a small, balding, slightly monkeyish man, bossed around and silenced by both his wife and his son, slowly formed in his mind. His Fairfield grandfather was certainly nothing like Quando.

"You can't possibly remember much about him," said Mrs.

Fairfield. "And we don't seem to talk about the Fairfield side of the family, what with the grandparents being dead now and your dad gone off to God knows where. But I suppose I should make myself remember them. After all, they are your ancestors, every bit as much as my side of the family." She peered into her cup of tea as if she might read a fortune in it. "Not that I ever got on with your father's mother. She was a real bitch, though perhaps I shouldn't say it. For instance, I don't think she ever let your father be what he really wanted to be."

"Might have been a smart move! Because what did he want to be?" asked Roland, intrigued to hear his mother swearing. Midnight seemed to have released her from having to set Danny and Martin a good example.

"I don't know. Well, *he* didn't know himself. I mean, he did really well in that door maintenance business, and I'm not saying anything against it. But when you're a kid and people ask you what you want to be, you don't say, 'A door maintenance expert!' do you? Anyhow, your father was always, well, *limp* about his work. His mother was the one who did all the boasting."

"Did his father boast too?" asked Roland. He already knew the answer to that question but wanted to edge the conversation back to his shy grandfather once more.

"His old man was a good sort."

"A magician," said Roland, still trying to get her back on track. "You mean, he did tricks? Pulled flags out of his nose and so on?"

"Nothing like that," his mother replied scornfully. "It was a clairvoyant sort of thing. Extrasensory! Every now and then he could be a little bit spooky. I remember—oh, it was years ago, just after you were born, because of course I was boasting about you and so on, and I happened to say, jokingly, you know, that one of each would be lovely, and I would have a girl next time. But your grandfather shook his head and said I would have two more boys. Your father groaned and said one was enough to go on with, but the old man grinned back, a little bit nastily, which was rare for him, and told your dad *he* had nothing to worry about—none of his kids would ever bother him much . . . he'd be too busy rushing through doors and then locking them behind him. It didn't make much sense at the time, but when you come to think of it—"

"But anyone could say things like that," Roland interrupted rather scornfully, "and some of them would have a good chance of turning out to be more or less true."

"Maybe," said his mother, "but there were a lot of other things as well. I mean, just before your dad and I were married, the old man took me aside and said he would like to give me a secret wedding present. . . ."

Mrs. Fairfield broke off. Now that he was sitting opposite her, Roland could just make out, by the light of the heater, that she wore an uncertain smile that was sly, shy, and a little foolish, all at once.

"Go on!" he said, making himself sound impatient, when really he was filled with something closer to alarm.

"It sounds so silly," his mother said with a sigh. "Well, he asked me what I would like to *dream* about, and *I* said I'd like to dream about a garden. *The Secret Garden* had been my favorite book when I was about ten, and I'd always wanted a garden for myself, but there we were—your dad and me—starting off in an apartment one floor up with a balcony as big as a tea tray. So a garden just wasn't on!"

"Don't tell me!" exclaimed Roland derisively. "You had this great dream about a beautiful, perfectly weeded garden full of roses."

"Oh, I did. And I still dream about it," Mrs. Fairfield replied with unexpected spirit, "so don't get too smart about it. And it's not perfectly weeded. If I don't weed it, it can be a very weedy garden, particularly in springtime."

"You've never mentioned any dream garden," said Roland, rather accusingly.

"Not to you, maybe, but I do tell Danny," said his mother. "He knows about it. 'Are the violets in flower?' he asks, and, 'Have the poppies taken off?' And I tell him."

"*Danny* does?" cried Roland. "How come you've told Danny and never said a thing to me?"

"Look at the way you're behaving now that I *am* telling you!" his mother said crisply. "You're cross with me, aren't you? And besides, you're not interested in gardening. Danny is, though he doesn't talk about it."

"I'm *interested,*" exclaimed Roland. "I'm interested in what you're telling me, though it sounds a bit—I don't know—sort of weird, really, and—"

His mother interrupted him. "It's not weird," she said indignantly. "And you were the one who brought up the subject of magicians. It's private—a private hobby I work on in my sleep every now and then. And I began telling Danny when he was about four. Remember how he used to get earaches? I used to sit up with him and tell him garden stories . . . tell him what was in flower and what I was pruning and—well, it's not worth going into it, really."

"But you make it sound as if it's a real garden," Roland persisted. "I mean, do the same flowers and things go on from dream to dream?"

"Well, they do," his mother said. "Every now and then—sometimes two nights running, sometimes weeks or even months apart—I dream I'm in this garden and it's . . . oh, some season. Spring or something! Anyhow, I wander around with a hoe in my hand, weeding and watering, setting out a few plants. There's a little greenhouse where I can put trays of seeds."

"And it's always the same one? The same garden?" Roland persisted.

"Oh, yes," said his mother. "And the plants I planted in dreams a few months ago might be coming into flower. I've seen the lilacs flower in late spring for years and years. And from somewhere outside the garden I can hear the sound of the sea. Funny, isn't it?"

"You should have a real garden," declared Roland, made restless by the discovery that his mother, who apparently longed to have a garden, lived in a house with nothing more than a big lawn and three oleander trees in front of it and a small vegetable patch at the back. But she laughed and shook her head at him.

"Look, I've got my parsley, silver beets, and broccoli," she said, "and anyway, I haven't much time to garden. I mean, it's a hellishly busy life, what with running the business as well as the house, and keeping an eye on you three kids. So I only garden in that dream your grandfather gave me. That's fine by me. He did a few other things too, when he got the chance, but as I said, your grandmother used to be angry if she caught him at it. She called him an old cheat, but I like to think he did have a secret power . . . a gentle little power that was all his own."

"You've never said anything about it before," said Roland reproachfully.

"Well, you've never asked me. And besides, I don't think about it much," she said reflectively. "It isn't often that it pops into my head as it did just now. And your father took after his mother in some ways. He certainly didn't like it talked about."

"Didn't like it . . . what do you mean?" asked Roland. His heart began thumping in expectation of some strange revelation.

"If ever the old man made any joke about having second sight or anything, which he did from time to time when his wife wasn't listening," said Mrs. Fairfield, "your father would look fed up. Sometimes he'd get really angry. He'd say the old man was away with the fairies."

"Trickery!" suggested Roland, copying a voice he remembered, and his mother looked over at him, obviously taken aback by the imitation.

"Oh, you *do* remember," she said. "You sounded just like him then."

"I think I dream his voice from time to time," Roland said. "or perhaps I remember it. Sometimes its hard to tell the difference between dreaming and remembering."

"The strange thing is . . . ," Mrs. Fairfield went on, "the *really* strange thing is that I think your father might have had the same kind of power himself, only I think his mother might have terrified it out of him when he was just a boy. Well, no! I don't mean really *out* of him! If I'm right, it was still there, working away in him. But I'm pretty sure she might have made him fight against it. And I think fighting against it sort of . . . detached him . . . broke him off from life, which meant breaking him off from me and you kids in the end. But that's just a loony theory I have tucked away in the back of my head. I suppose I'd rather he ran off because he was screwed up about himself than because he'd lost interest in us. Of course, I've never known for sure. And I'll never know now."

"Maybe not," said Roland.

But his mother went on, working it out for herself rather than for him. "In the beginning his being a bit off center didn't show, but the years went by and he grew more—I don't know—more distracted, always wrestling with something inside himself. I know he didn't leave us for any of the usual reasons. There wasn't another woman or anything like that. It was because he was haunted. . . ." But here she broke off and looked toward Roland, making a comical face, as if she wanted to make fun of the ridiculous things she was saying. "Well, that's my theory. He ran to keep ahead of his ghosts."

"It doesn't make sense," said Roland slowly.

"No, it doesn't, does it?" agreed his mother. "But a lot of things don't." She paused. "I still wonder about him, you know, wonder if he's keeping ahead of the ghosts. And I know he wonders about us."

"He's never once sent me even a birthday card," said Roland bitterly.

"I *know* he wonders," Mrs. Fairfield repeated. "He loved me. I know he did. And he absolutely loved you, too—"

"He loved us all so much he took off and was never heard of again," Roland finished the story for her.

"He was a driven man," his mother said.

"Yeah! Driven by taxi! He did take a taxi to the airport, didn't he?" said Roland.

"Well, I'm a lucky woman," said Mrs. Fairfield. "At least I have you."

Ten minutes later, after a quick, sharp shower, Roland was sitting at his desk in his bathrobe working hard on his last two assignments. At 3 A.M. he reset the alarm, leaving the clock on his desk. *When it goes off, I'll have to walk over to the desk to turn it off, and that'll wake me up,* he thought. Pulling back the quilt, he climbed into bed between clean, cool sheets. *Sleep,* he thought, *real sleep, this time. And if I dream about a garden, well, I'll . . . I'll just laugh and keep on walking. And I'll make up my mind about things tomorrow—no, later on this morning. What is that* sound? *What* is *that sound? It isn't a sound though, is it? What have I turned into? What am I becoming? No! I won't think about it now. And after all, I might wake up to find everything's gone quiet once more. Let's hope!* He let his head fall onto the pillows. Sleep! True sleep took him in at last, and he did not dream any dreams that he could remember.

A Dangerous End to an Ordinary Day

The alarm screamed out urgently, and Roland woke for the second time in the same morning, swore, flung back the quilt, and leaped toward his desk. It had been a confused and troubled man who had fallen asleep four hours earlier. It was a fierce and determined one who turned the alarm off and then stood quite still, frowning and blinking.

I've just had *it with all this Jess Ferret shit!* he thought, then said it aloud so that he could actually hear himself saying it. The sound of the words, the shape they took, swimming inside his head, made him feel in charge of himself once more. He began to dress with particular care, and when, at last, he glanced in the mirror, it was not an altered version of his father he saw, but a perfectly organized Crichton-prefect image.

"No one's going to drive us apart," Roland murmured to his reflection. "We'll stick together, you and me! I'll be a good prefect, and you be a good reflection. And I'll concentrate on Chris. She deserves the best. Like, she deserves *you,* which is to say *me,*" he mumbled on, pleased with the way the words were imposing themselves over the sound that was not a sound. "Well, *me* the way I'm going to be from now on. I'll tell Mr. Hudson that Jess's parents are away and that she—"

"Hey! Roley's lost it at last," yelled Danny, peering in at the open door. "He's talking to himself."

"What's he saying?" Martin called, and came to stare through the door as well.

Roland looked at their sharp, bright faces and knew they were anticipating some kind of brotherly abuse. He took a breath.

"I was just saying what good brothers you are and how lucky I am to have you," he said in a syrupy voice. Danny and Martin stood staring at him, grins fixing, then fading. Their frowning eyebrows and open mouths expressed a sort of puzzled disappointment. Triumphantly, he strolled past them, making for the kitchen.

"You were *not* saying that," Danny shouted after him. "I know you weren't."

Out in the kitchen Roland dropped an arm around his mother's shoulders and placed the parody of a tender kiss beside her ear. He knew she would understand that he was remembering their midnight conversation and was letting her know that, even with blatant morning sunlight beating in through every eastern window, it was still being appreciated.

"Darling boy," said his mother. "We don't get enough chances to sit down and talk to each other, do we? Oh, by the way, I forgot to tell you that Chris rang you earlier last night."

Roland, pouring milk onto muesli, barely looked up. His mother was now speaking in that familiar motherly voice—a slightly accusing one.

"Oh?" he asked.

"Well, I thought she sounded just a little bit *hurt,*" his mother replied.

Roland cast a defiant but apprehensive look toward the phone. "Hurt *and* annoyed!" his mother added.

"I haven't done anything wrong," Roland said.

"She asked if you could ring her back," said his mother. "But you were home late-ish. Where were you, by the way? I thought you must be with her, but if you weren't . . ."

"I shot round to Jess Ferret's," Roland said. "She had a book I wanted to borrow, and we . . . we started arguing about politics."

"Oh, that Ferret girl!" exclaimed Mrs. Fairfield. "Oh well!" She sounded relieved, perfectly sure, no doubt, that Jess was nothing for the beautiful daughter of a councillor to worry over. But then she added, "Roland, I like Chris. I don't want to think you're—"

"That I'm what?" asked Roland aggressively.

"That you might be taking her for granted, that's what," said his mother briskly. "I don't expect you to stick together forever—you're too young for that—but I want you to treat her fairly and—"

"Go on! Tell me again," said Roland. "About you and the old man! You started going out together when you were at school, and you stuck together until he got bored or haunted or—"

"Well, we did stick together," said his mother. "We stuck together for years and years, which a lot of people don't, and those years still *mean* something. I know what I'm talking about, and I want you to behave reasonably."

"Reason-ably!" called Danny from beside the hearth, assuming a mincing English accent. "Behave reason-ably!"

"Nice-ly!" echoed Martin mockingly from the next room.

Roland ignored this. He had had a lot of practice ignoring Danny and Martin.

"I want you to treat your girlfriends well. Are you *listening* to me?" said his mother. Roland went to the fridge to get the yogurt he had opened yesterday morning. There it was. He looked into the fridge with pleasure, delighted to notice, there in the bottom drawer, lettuce that was slightly wilted. For some reason this fault made morning life seem particularly real. Long live the embracing imperfection of things that seemed to be drawing him back to real life once more. Faults were precious to him.

"Oh, well," said his mother impatiently, "time's ticking by. Get what you want, and get out of my way. You take up so much room these days."

"You can't have too much of a good thing," said Roland,

snatching the yogurt and heading back to his breakfast bowl once more.

Later, at school, he talked and joked with Chris, and with Tom and Stephen, and he did not once allow himself to look over their shoulders, not even when Jess appeared and went to her place as quietly as usual. In class he listened intently to the teachers, volunteered to answer questions, and joined in discussions. He smiled briefly but boldly at Mr. Hudson during the literature session, ignoring the persistent, quizzical tilting of the Hudson eyebrows, and looking quickly away in case their eyes met and Mr. Hudson got some hint of inner alteration in progress.

"Where were you last night?" asked Chris, not so much sourly as accusingly.

Roland met her gaze fearlessly, wondering as he did so if she was convinced by his hearty imitation of his usual self. Just for a moment his determination wavered. He needed to convince other people in order to convince himself, for at the moment his acting was more for his own benefit than anyone else's. He must expect to quaver in and out of everyday life just a little, because . . . because . . . No! He mustn't let himself so much as *speculate* about any of *that* for a while. It was all there—crouching, ready to sweep in on him, ready to swallow him and make him part of that endless sigh. But perhaps the trick lay in simply refusing to listen. Thinking about the dark state that had taken him over the evening before would only give it power over him.

"Something's happened to you," Chris said, "and you're not letting on."

"Nothing much," said Roland. "I'm just having a screwed-up time at home. You know."

"Your mother sounded fine," said Chris. "Except she didn't know where you were. Well, she *said* she didn't. Was she just covering up?"

They were walking side by side into school for their first afternoon classes. Roland stopped and turned to face her.

"Look—what's the big deal?" he asked. "I keep telling you, I'm just the same as I usually am."

"Do you know what?" said Chris. "I don't believe you. I can see your little wheels going *whizzz*!" She pointed her index finger at him and rolled it around and around in the air. "You need miles more practice at being a liar."

She hurried ahead of him to the back door of the school, turned, smiled briefly, and then vanished. Her first afternoon class was French; his was history of art. They were bound in opposite directions.

For all her smiling, Roland knew he had upset her, that she was not brokenhearted, but certainly hurt. Hurt—yes—and angry beneath her smile. Roland stared after her, and the feeling he had been trying to create—the feeling that the day was just another day—began to shiver out of line.

But then he forced the shivering to stop. He made himself remember the times when the world—when his home—had seemed as if it might be about to shiver itself to bits and fall away. He remembered how his mother would put on a bright smile and say, "Let's read a story!" Just after his father left, she had made and remade a reliable everyday world for him. It could be done. It was a family tradition. "Let's tell a story," he muttered. "A good one!" And, saying this, he dived in at the back door of the school, to run, light footed, after Chris, catching her just before she turned in at her classroom door.

"Hey, Chris, it's just that I don't always want to be *grilled* about everything," he said. "I get enough of that from my mum."

Sure enough, Chris looked startled, then a little thoughtful, because, of course, she would not want to think she was behaving like anyone's mother.

"I'll think that over," she said, then added, "I'm being terribly fair to you. Hope you appreciate it."

"But what have I *done*?" he wanted to demand, though he already knew. Over the last few days he had been listening to voices other than hers. He had started looking past her. She was the sort of girl who'd notice a thing like that, and she wouldn't put up with it—not for a minute.

The rest of the day went past smoothly enough. It was Roland's turn to do his prefect after-school duties. He watched Chris and Stephen leave together and Tom bike away, but he was as true to his official obligations as he usually was.

There had, of course, been times during that day when he couldn't help being aware of Jess, but he refused to acknowledge her. If, coming or going, he found himself accidentally looking at her, he simply let his gaze slip over her as if she were something that he didn't need to think about—like a chair, a window, or a passing dog. He refused to identify her, even to himself. At one time during the afternoon he had caught himself wondering if by any chance she was looking at him, and found he had no idea. Good! That had to be good. He must cut himself free from the possibilities that seemed to erupt around Jess Ferret; he must disengage himself. After all, once upon a time (a week ago), ignoring her had been automatic. By tomorrow or the next day, if he worked at it, it might become automatic once more.

Duties done, he collected his pack and then his bike and made for Chris's house, only to find Chris and Stephen sitting together, listening to a tape of a New Zealand band that had recently been praised in Australia. When it was finished and they had talked about it thoroughly, Stephen still hung around, though Roland reckoned any reasonably tactful friend would have shot off and left him alone with Chris. After all, her mother would be home soon. At last Stephen picked up the unspoken hints, a little reluctantly perhaps, and left, promising that he would see them tomorrow. Chris promptly slid another tape into her tape recorder and turned up the sound a little. Then she plumped herself down beside Roland, turning to face him as she did so.

"Well," she said. "Here we are again—at last." Roland made a sound that took him by surprise—a sort of groan, almost as if he were in pain—as he rolled toward her. Just briefly he had the impression that she might have tried to lean back from him, but if so, he was too quick for her. At any rate, when he put his arms around her, she certainly flung hers around him, apparently with relief and abandon. He kissed her and kissed her, as if he were cracking up with thirst and she were a fountain from which he must drink, while she ran her fingers over the back of his neck and into his hair, pressing his face down on hers, apparently every bit as passionate as he was. Yet when they broke apart, panting a little, her expression took him by surprise. She was not looking at him with the melting, breathless look he had expected to see—indeed, had seen on other occasions—but in a much cooler way. Calculating, really.

"Nice!" she said, nodding thoughtfully and giving him her slanting sideways glance.

"How about 'terrific'?" suggested Roland, astonished to find that he, too, was cooler than he had somehow imagined himself to be. He had planned to surrender to passion, something which, up until now, had always been easy to do. Perhaps the calculation he was seeing in Chris was something reflecting from him.

"Listen, Roley!" said Chris. "Just tell me! What's happened to you?"

"Nothing!" Roland said impatiently. "Don't keep on at me. Nothing's happened! Nothing!"

"I'm not dumb," Chris cried back angrily. And then they began kissing desperately, because questions and answers were useless, and kissing might be a way of avoiding them. Just for a moment he thought he might truly be about to fuse back into what he *had* been, but Chris pushed him away.

"You've been different all this week," she said. "I've been thinking you must be going off me." She sounded genuinely astonished by the possibility. "You behave as though you're really thinking of something more important than . . . than anything that's going on around you. Including me! And today—well, I've only got to look at you! Are you *on* something?"

"Don't be crazy," said Roland angrily. "If I had been shooting up, I'd probably boast about it."

And then, with something like relief, he heard the sound of footsteps in the sitting room. Chris's mother was home and shouting cheerfully, almost at once, that they were to turn that damned noise down.

Chris moved to her player, turned the sound down the merest fraction, and then went to open the door.

"We're here," she called aloud. "You've really changed," she hissed back over her shoulder. "Is it anything to do with . . ."

Roland held his breath. If she mentioned—if she so much as mentioned . . . He fought against naming Jess even to himself, thinking that if he had to say her name aloud, the whole carefully protected day, already precarious, would fall to pieces. But Chris didn't finish her sentence.

"Would you two like a sherry?" called Chris's mother. She was proud of treating her daughter's friends as if they were mature adults. "Or a beer? There's beer in the fridge."

"Thanks, but I've got to go," said Roland. "Offer me two next time."

One step at a time, he told himself, biking home. *That's the important thing. One step . . . one step . . . then another . . .* But in spite of all his efforts, he was on the edge, and now that he was on his own and out in the world, there was the breathing and roaring and chattering and singing once again. *Breaking apart,* it was saying. *Breaking apart . . . melting together . . . feeding . . . falling . . . flowing . . . flowering . . . folding . . . singing . . . stalking . . . circling . . . circling . . . circling.*

And then he was home. Danny and Martin bounced around him as he came in, insulting him at the first opportunity. Well, he was used to that. Besides, in his present mood he found himself able to see quite clearly that their mockery was their way of trying to be grown up—to be his equal. They both believed that insults would engage his attention. So he responded by insulting them both, smiling as he did so, and they were delighted, shouting cheerful abuse back at him until their mother came out of the kitchen, telling them to be quiet. She was sick, she cried, of their rough, noisy behavior.

At that moment the phone rang, and Roland sprang toward it, anxious to reassure Chris, though not quite sure just what he would be reassuring her about.

"It's me," said a voice. He had never spoken to Jess over the phone, but he immediately knew who it was. "I want to talk to you."

"Hey! What's happened to all that 'I vant to be alone!' stuff?" he asked derisively.

His mother turned toward him, her mouth open, obviously gearing herself up to give him good advice.

"I just want to talk to you," Jess repeated.

"Now it's me who wants to be alone," he replied. "I've sort of worked out that your scene's not my scene. I'm keen to live with that."

"Yes," she said, "but from now on my scene just *is* your scene. It always will be. No way out! Not for you! Not for me." He thought her voice sounded tight and even trembling, but the truth of what she was saying crashed through all the feeble struggles of his day. Pretense! That whole day had been nothing but pretense. In a moment he was right back to where he had been the night before. "If you don't talk to me, I'll work myself into your dreams," Jess promised in a sinister voice.

Roland believed she might be able to do this. The possibility horrified him. All the same, it was the tremble in her voice that most truly caught his attention.

"Is something wrong?" he asked rather more gently, while his mother smiled and nodded across the room at him.

"I'm sorry I got so angry with you last night," she said.

"Hey! No problemo!" said Roland, keeping a wary eye on his mother.

"I just don't know what to do," said Jess across the distance. "It's silly to ask if I can trust you. You're bound to say I can, and you might even believe it. Well, I might even believe it too."

"I'd never say that," declared Roland. "You *can't* trust me. And anyhow, I can't talk about it, right? Hovering parents."

"I'm not hovering," said his mother crossly. "This happens to be the family living room, just in case you forgot."

"Blast!" he heard Jess muttering, but to herself rather than to him. "Oh, damn and blast! Blam and dast!"

"What's wrong?" he cried, wondering for a terrible moment if the creature might be sliding through Jess into the phone lines and shooting across the city, eager to pour itself in at his ear and repossess his vulnerable head. "Shall I come round?" he asked in spite of his fear.

"No! Don't come here!" she said quickly. "Not here." She was really frightened, he thought. "I'll meet you in the mall," she suggested. "We'll maul each other there," she added, trying to joke.

"What's wrong with your place?" he asked. "After all, the worst has happened, hasn't it?"

"I want to meet somewhere else," she said in a barely audible voice. "How about the museum?" she then asked rather more confidently.

"It'll be closed by the time we get there," Roland replied. There was a silence as Jess considered this.

"Tomorrow morning?" she suggested at last.

They were bargaining—like people in a market. Roland made another face. He hated the thought of organizing his life simply to suit Jess Ferret. Yet he was so relieved to find himself talking to her once more that he was angry with himself all over again.

"Tomorrow afternoon, then," he said, bargaining so that he wouldn't be the one to give in. "Early!" he added, and thought he could actually hear her hesitating, as if her hesitation had a sound that carried over the wires.

"Okay! Fine!" she exclaimed at last. "In front of the polar bear. Early afternoon! Say about one thirty."

"I don't know what you think I can do about anything," he began, suddenly horrified to realize that after all his efforts to work his way back to his previous, plain existence, that other haunted life was claiming him so effortlessly. He took a breath, planning to say he had changed his mind.

But perhaps Jess had anticipated this. She hung up abruptly, and the sound at the other end of the line was so violent that *hanging up* seemed too mild a term. It sounded as if the slammed phone might fall to pieces.

"How was she?" his mother called. She had been listening shamelessly, sure that he was talking to Chris.

"She's fine," said Roland. "We were just fixing up a date for tomorrow."

His mother gave him that sly, shy look, relieved and oddly flirtatious.

"Have you two been having a lover's quarrel?" she asked.

"Oh, Mum!" exclaimed Roland yet again, shaking his head in disgust. "Just forget it!"

"Hey," Martin called to Danny. "Roley and Chris are having a fight!"

"Now see what you've done," Roland cried. "When can I get to have a phone in my room? Or a cell phone? Living here is like living on a bloody stage with no curtain and everyone clapping or booing me every minute."

"Booing you, mostly!" cried Danny.

And a sort of irritated relief flooded through Roland. Brotherly abuse made it seem as if a true family life was being lived once more.

INNER SILENCE

Saturday. Yes, Saturday again, already. A week ago he had been . . . but he mustn't think of that. Roland did the things he usually did, still trying to remind himself what it was like to be an average man in an average world . . . trying to locate the foundation of that life he had carefully constructed the day before. However, all the things that had happened yesterday already felt like incidents in a ghost life. He was changed and still changing, and there was nothing he could do about it. For one thing, he was suddenly wondering why his private inner voice—the one that had spoken from deep in his head for so many years—had fallen silent. He found to his surprise that, though its nagging advice and urgent warnings had often irritated him, he was missing it.

Roland grimaced. Invaded, he thought. And by now that invader was welcoming every breath he drew into his lungs, monitoring every drop of blood as it surged through the left-right gates of his heart, and insisting that he honor the endless sigh. Perhaps the invader within was not an invader after all, but was simply part of him, newly awake, raising its head and demanding his attention.

"Are you okay?" asked his mother, looking through his open bedroom door.

"Of course," he replied, a little irritably. "Can't I even *think* around here without someone creeping up behind me?"

"Sorry," she said, though sounding pleased rather than really sorry. "It's just that you've been looking a bit distracted over the last day or two. I noticed it the other night, actually, but I thought it was just—you know—midnight. I suppose midnight gets to us all."

"I was just *thinking,*" Roland said obstinately, remembering how Chris had accused him of looking weird. "Isn't that allowed anymore? Oh, shit! So *sorry*!"

"That's enough of that," said his mother. "Danny and Martin might hear you."

"Just suppose *I* listened to them," Roland said, grinning in spite of his irritation. "Then you'd really have something to worry about. Those two make me sound like a beginner when it comes to dirty language."

He struggled on through the morning, frowning and muttering alternate encouragements and warnings to himself. And in between other things he did call Chris—called her twice. She was not at home.

"Damn! Damn! Damn!" he breathed, grinning again, but a rather different grin this time. It felt hard and unamused, because when her mother told him she was out, what he had mainly felt was relief. He caught himself thinking, before he could stop himself, that Chris was irrelevant.

Roland ate a quick lunch with his family.

"It's a cold day," said his mother, still imagining he was going to meet Chris. "You can take the car. But for God's sake, be careful! The traffic's mad on a Saturday."

"He'll be part of the madness," said Danny.

"If he hits someone, he'll kill them," cried Martin, rather as if he were looking forward to it.

"As long as he isn't killed himself," said their mother. "That's all I care about. Anyway," she added, "he won't hit anyone. He's a careful driver." Saying this, she fixed him with a commanding gaze, as if she could force him to be a good driver simply by looking at him in the right way.

MEETING IN THE MUSEUM

Roland set off into the early afternoon, responsible and levelheaded, making way generously for turning traffic and allowing the proper distance between his own car and any cars in front of him.

The oldest part of the museum resembled a castle of brownish stone, its high roof crenellated, its doorway fronted by four fluted marble pillars. Recent extensions swelled up and out behind it, hatching triumphantly from that first stone shell. His father had been fond of the museum, he remembered, and they had often gone there together when he was a small boy.

He pulled into the museum parking lot, not getting out of the car immediately, but leaning forward on the steering wheel as he tried to guess, not for the first time, why Jess had been so opposed to meeting him at her house. Her house! Jess owned her own house—a house that, he now felt, owned him. Were there other, still stranger secrets behind the green door—secrets she wanted to keep to herself? And had he been right in thinking he could detect something like fear in her voice when he suggested meeting her there? Questions! Questions! Life was nothing but questions with smudgy answers, or no answers at all.

Then at last, sighing a little, like someone who feels he might be about to take on new burdens, he climbed out of the car and walked toward the pillared entrance and in past the front desk. "This way, sport!" he muttered to himself. ("This way, sport!" he remembered his father saying, somewhere in the distant past. It was irritating that even his voice no longer seemed to be entirely his own.) Relieved that the museum spaces were largely empty, probably because it was so early in the afternoon, he strolled along a walkway lined with glass cases in which a variety of animals were displayed in dramatic attitudes against curved dioramic backgrounds.

And there, in front of the Arctic case, studying a polar bear that was poised to advance threateningly on two seals, stood Jess Ferret. Perhaps the bear managed to let her know that Roland was coming up behind her, for as he caught sight of her back and her bad haircut she turned in a businesslike way, just as if she knew he was there.

"Hi," he said, lifting his hand in a vague greeting, but Jess did not respond in kind.

"We can't stand and talk here," she said abruptly. "There's somewhere to sit in front of the museum café. I checked it out. Come on."

"But then I won't be able to watch the polar bear," Roland said. "It looks as if it's been waiting for me."

"Well, you'll be able to watch the lions instead," she replied. Her closed smile was perfunctory—an imitation of itself.

"What's wrong?" asked Roland cautiously.

"Nothing," she said airily, but he knew she was lying.

As they walked on he studied her in a sly, sideways fashion. Where was the shine and buoyancy that had transformed her last Saturday? Did she light up like that only when she was safely behind her own green door? Today, walking stiffly between cases of stiffly angled, long-dead animals, she certainly seemed reduced.

The museum café came into sight on the right, but they turned left into a little alcove furnished with soft chairs that was unexpectedly empty. Clearly visible from where they were sitting was a case in which they could see a lion and lioness, both slightly moth eaten around their muzzles, looking down with glassy affection at two playful cubs and still holding the precise attitudes he remembered from his childhood visits.

"Coffee? Tea?" Jess asked him. "My shout."

"Just water," Roland replied. "I'm really thirsty."

Jess crossed over to the café and came back with a tray holding a jug of water clinking with ice cubes, which she lowered carefully onto the low table between them. Roland, watching her pour water into two long glasses, was reminded, rather uneasily, of Quando pouring wine in the blue-and-silver café. Quickly putting the image out of his head, he cleared his throat a little.

WHAT THE LIONS HEARD

"Here we are," he said invitingly. But Jess was silent. "So?" he persisted. "What do you want to tell me?"

She answered his question with one of her own. "Were you scared?"

"Scared? Me? What of?"

"You know what I mean," she said. "At my place the other night. Something happened, didn't it? You saw the eidolon."

"The what?"

Jess gave him an impatient look.

"Don't muck about," she begged him. "The eidolon. That means a sort of image or spirit. But anyhow, I know *you* know what I'm talking about."

Roland gave in.

"I called it the creature," he said. And he was immediately flooded with huge relief as, here in this little alcove, in front of the lions, he gave up trying to force himself back into an earlier state. Ease flooded through him as he finally admitted to himself that, try as he might, he would never again be what he had been this time two days ago. That man was gone forever. "Are you making out your house is haunted? Or that you're some sort of a witch?"

"No!" she cried almost angrily. "I'm a scientist. I connect with things. I feel my way into them." Then her clenched hands relaxed and her mouth drooped. (Absentmindedly Roland thought she had beautiful lips.) "I'm a *sort* of scientist," she repeated wearily, "but part of my science is *old.* It ties up with alchemy." She threw the word at him as if she were anticipating derision.

Roland longed to cry out jeeringly, "Oh, sure! Sure! And I'm Einstein!" But he remembered the advance of the creature and felt, once more, the explosion of its passage through him. Pushing the memory to one side, he tried to recall the definition of alchemy he had read in the *World Book Dictionary* at school. To his amazement (just as if he had turned on a switch), the words lit up in his head: *"Alchemy dealt not only with the mysteries of matter, but also with those of creation and life. It sought to harmonize the human individual with the universe around him."* For some reason this unnaturally accurate memory of the dictionary definition frightened him, although he could not reject it.

"Are you making out you can turn tin into gold or something?" he asked, trying to hide his moment of confusion with deliberate provocation.

"No!" Jess exclaimed indignantly. "Mind you, we did think a lot about transmutation," she added.

"We?" asked Roland. "You and who?"

Jess sighed.

"Me and my dad," she said in the voice of someone admitting a fault. "In the beginning, that is." She broke off, her face brightening. "Isaac Newton believed in alchemy," she cried, as if this must convince him of its authenticity. "He was one of the greatest scientists ever, but he was an alchemist as well. He probably believed that matter and spirit were interchangeable, and in a funny way that's part of what physicists believe today, isn't it?"

"Whoa! You've lost me," said Roland, screwing up his face doubtfully.

"Well, of course we don't think of matter and spirit in the same way as Newton did," admitted Jess. "But what if I said that matter and energy were different forms of the same thing? An atom used to be the tiniest piece of matter that we could work our way down to, but these days we can go even farther in, and guess what? The atom—matter, that is—is mostly space. We've got the nucleus with electrons and neutrons dancing around it, right?"

"It's not quite my scene," said Roland cautiously, "but yes, they do say something like that. You're probably right!"

"When we get that far in, we're not dealing with stuff . . . not with matter in the way we usually think of matter," Jess said with unexpected confidence. Roland could tell she was repeating something she had often thought about. "It's all forces and relationships—spirit, in a way. Henry More thought a single spirit underlay everything, and these days that could be a sort of image—a metaphor, say, of what people like Stephen Hawking are getting at when they talk about unifying the forces, gravity and the electromagnetic forces and all that."

Her expression changed as she spoke. The anxiety that had haunted her when she first turned toward him was fading. She smiled, not so much at him as at an idea that thrilled her. Roland watched, fascinated.

"Henry Moore? That sculptor who did those great, lumpy shapes?" he asked, pleased he could flush out odd pieces of knowledge, which were so useful in tying conversations back into a real world that everyone agreed upon.

"Nah!" said Jess scornfully. "Not that one. The Henry More I'm talking about was a friend of Newton's. He looked after Newton a bit when Newton first went to university in Cambridge."

"So are you saying that science and alchemy are the same thing?" he asked her.

"No!" she said slowly. "No! Look! Just give me a moment." Bowing her head, she frowned down at her own clasped hands, seeming to think very carefully. Then she looked up and began to speak as if she were telling him a story.

"Once there were—let's say there were—magicians, but

not quite what we mean these days when we talk about magicians," she said. "Once there was another way of understanding the world. It wasn't through reason, not even through poetry . . . it was through—I don't know—a sort of *sympathy.*" She leaned her elbow on the arm of her chair and, resting her head on her hand, made a face as she struggled to find the right words. "Intuition?" she said, as if she were asking him.

"Right!" he muttered, nodding without knowing exactly what he was agreeing to.

"It was like having . . . like an extra sense. It still is, except that most people don't bother about it, and it withers away." She touched the center of her forehead. "A third eye," she suggested.

"Like the tuatara?" Roland said brightly, feeling it was time to say something positive, just to prove that he was following the explanation that she was trying so hard to give.

"No!" Jess said. "That's a real eye, even if it is covered with skin. It's got a lens, a retina, all that. The third eye I'm talking about meant that people who had it were able to see—no, not to *see,* to *apprehend* things that other people missed out on. And in a way it can be just as much a hand as an eye, because some of the people who have it—the apprehenders—can reach out and *nudge* the world a little. Well, scientists do their own sort of nudging, don't they? But the apprehenders can often nudge without any instrument except will."

"What?" asked Roland, frowning. "Are you saying there are people who can look at something on the other side of the room and sort of lure it over to them?"

"Some of them can do things like that," said Jess. His skeptical tone immediately made her defensive. "Psychokinesis, it's called! But that's just a trick. It's not the most wonderful thing about being an apprehender."

"Oh, come on!" said Roland. "If you can make things come across the room to you when you call . . ." He broke off. "Can *you* do that?"

A curious expression crossed Jess's face. She seemed as if she were being tempted to do something shameful. Then she grinned a little and looked past him; she blinked. It was a long blink.

"I can if I want to," she said, "but I don't often want to. I mean, I used to nudge things around when I was little, but—"

"Show me, then," demanded Roland.

"I have," said Jess. "You just haven't noticed it yet."

Roland looked left and right and into the air.

"What have you done?" he asked suspiciously.

Jess laughed. Roland was about to say that he didn't believe her, when he saw that there was a faint sheen of sweat on her forehead that certainly hadn't been there before.

"What I'm talking about is more of an art than science, I think," she said, speaking so readily that he knew she must have discussed it with herself over and over again. "But when it comes to shifting the world—actually moving it around, that is—science mostly works much better for more people, and besides, it can be taught. Nudging the world is exhausting. And what really matters with the talent I'm talking about is that it sort of *completes* you. You have to recognize it in yourself and move into it. Then you set it free, and you set yourself free too."

Then she fell silent, and they sat staring into each other's eyes, each waiting for the other to speak first. As they stared and waited a thin trickle of blood crept down from Jess's left nostril, and one hand dived into her patchwork bag, searching for a tissue.

"Are you bleeding because you've *done* something?" he demanded, and looked desperately at the table between them, studying the glasses of water and the melting ice, searching for some alteration before he ran his gaze around the alcove, the lions and the front of the café opposite.

"Oh, come on! What is it?" he cried impatiently. "Tell me!" He broke off. Behind the tissue, which she now held clasped to her nose, Jess was laughing at him.

"Anyhow, are you saying you're one of these magicians?" he demanded rather aggressively.

Jess crumpled the tissue and dropped it onto the tray. Once again their eyes met, and as they did this Jess's eyes contracted into black slits. Narrow though they were, Roland recognized a familiar darkness beyond them. He thought he could make out a glow of distant suns. He thought he saw himself, suspended among those remote pinpricks of light.

"I'm telling you that *you're* one," Jess replied.

"Suddenly? Just like that?" he asked. He tried to sound light about it, but his fingers trembled violently against the cold glass he was holding. He had to put it down before he dropped it.

"You always have been," she said. "I thought you'd never do anything about it. A lot of people don't. But now you really have to think about it. Because people who go as far as you've gone and don't face up to it ruin themselves."

(*I think your father could have been a bit of a magician himself,* Mrs. Fairfield's voice reminisced somewhere in Roland's head.

Trickery! said his father's voice distantly—ruining himself by saying such things, perhaps.)

"Oh! Come off it!" Roland exclaimed robustly. "What sort of new-age rubbish are you on about?"

"It's not new age," Jess said. "It's ancient. Forgotten. The magicians, the ones that are left, live secretly . . . secret from themselves most of the time. Dad and I, for example, we used to lead a double life. He lectured in physics at the university, but at home he played with his third-eye power." Roland now remembered walking along the hall in Jess's house on his first visit and looking into the room that had reminded him of the laboratory at school. "And he could, well, move the world to his advantage. Not that he did very often. It wasn't what interested him."

"Does—what did you call it—*nudging* the world always make your nose bleed?" asked Roland, glancing around again.

"No," said Jess. "The thing is . . ." She stopped, seeming to change her mind about what she had been about to say. "Nudging the world doesn't interest me in the way some other things do."

"But you're trying to make out it sort of overlaps with science?" asked Roland.

Jess sighed.

"What I'm talking about doesn't register," she said. "I mean, there are forces that everyone knows about that can be detected and measured . . . you know"—she sounded certain that Roland would know—"the force of gravity, the electromagnetic force, and the two nuclear forces, the strong force and the weak one." Roland nodded in agreement. "But the one I learned to play with," said Jess, "was like a sort of music you can't hear."

"Music you can't hear!" exclaimed Roland. "Must be just great!"

"It's a metaphor . . . like saying trumpets sound red and violins sound green," said Jess defensively. "I don't know how else to describe it. And anyhow, you must have some idea of it yourself." But Roland was not yet prepared to admit that he could hear—was hearing perpetually—the sound of the universe breathing.

"Your parents feel this too?" he asked. "I mean, is it something you inherit?"

He was thinking of his own father and grandfather. At the mention of her parents Jess's open expression closed off. She became guarded once more.

"Yes . . . they did feel it. I mean, they do. But they . . . they don't want to think about it in the way I do. And their lives—well, we live separate lives at present. They're off doing their own thing."

"What *is* their own thing?" he asked cautiously, remembering both her strange, still house and Mr. Hudson's questions. Jess fell silent and looked away from him.

"Okay," Roland said at last, "if you had told me any of this a few days ago, I'd have thought you were raving. But last night I did see that . . . what did you call it . . . that eidolon. That creature. In some ways it looked like you," he added, asking her a question by telling her something.

Once again silence fell between them.

"It *is* part of me," Jess admitted at last. "I've turned into my own ghost. I haunt myself. I did something that . . . but I don't want to talk about that right now."

"Well, do you want to talk about why your house feels so

weird?" he asked. "And why aren't your parents taking it in turns to be there, looking after you like a good mum and dad?"

"Why aren't yours looking after you?" Jess hissed back at him.

"There's only my mum," Roland said. "And when I go home, it *is* a home. Okay, so my mother fusses over me a bit too much. Okay, so my brothers and I fight. Things get disarranged and fall to bits and all that. But it's not like living in some sort of science-fiction suspended-animation state."

"My parents are allowed to live their own lives," said Jess stonily.

Roland abandoned the argument.

"My turn to tell *you* something," he said at last. "I don't even know that it's connected, but it feels as if it might be in a spooky way. And anyway, if I tell you something, we'll know each other's secrets. We'll be even." Leaning forward across the low table, his eyes fixed on her face, he told her about his shoplifting adventure.

"That *is* a bit peculiar," said Jess at last, looking at him in a puzzled way. "It doesn't sound like you. You're such a goody-goody. Why on earth did you do it?"

"I don't know," said Roland, irritated at being defined as a goody-goody, "but it feels connected to what's been going on over the last week or so. That's why I'm telling you."

"But why did that make you start talking to me?" she asked shrewdly. "Suddenly? Out of the blue?"

Roland's heart sank, but he knew that this time there could be no jokes and no evasion, either.

"I'm coming to that," he said. "Not that I want to, but . . . I was blackmailed into doing it. You see, someone saw me doing that shoplifting. Actually, by now I wonder if he didn't make me do it in some way. Because the things I stole match up with things I was given ages ago when I was a little kid. The person who gave them to me back then was a bit of a weirdo, and he's still around, so—"

"What person?" demanded Jess. She looked alarmed—more than alarmed. Suddenly, Roland thought, she looked terrified.

He leaned forward, lowering his voice. "I'll tell you all that in a minute. The thing is, I think this weirdo told someone else about what I'd done, and arranged for the other person to get hold of me and make out he was worried about you and to tell me that unless I made friends with you and found out what was wrong, he'd go to the principal about my shoplifting. Sorry it sounds so complicated," he added.

"Who blackmailed you?" cried Jess.

"It mattered this time last week," said Roland. "Now I don't care much."

"Who was it?" asked Jess again.

"Old Hudson," Roland told her. "I mean, in the beginning I thought he really *was* worried about you. But since then . . ." He stopped. Jess's expression was filled not only with fury, but with fear as well. "What's wrong?" hissed Roland in an agony of apprehension.

"Old Hudson?" Jess exclaimed in a voice that was soft but also violent. "He's got a brother who . . . a brother who's like me! Like you! A brother who's one of us, but—"

"The politician brother?" asked Roland, interrupting her.

"He's more than a politician," replied Jess. "He's more than an apprehender. He's a collector."

"A collector?" asked Roland.

"He wants it all," she declared aloud, and then, at the sound of her own voice, looked around in consternation, as if her very words might be pulled out of the air and used against her. "He wants to own it all," she repeated in a whisper. And Roland suddenly knew—knew for certain—that Mr. Hudson's politician brother had another and very different identity.

"This brother . . . is he . . . are you talking about Quando? Quando the Magician?" he whispered back.

"Quando!" she echoed. "Yes! Tyrone Hudson's his true name. He was a magician . . . years ago, that is. And yes—he *is* a politician now, though he still puts on shows for children occasionally. Fun for the kiddies. Has he been trying to collect from you, too?"

"What does he collect?"

"He collects other people's power," Jess answered. "Has he been trying to collect from you, too?" she repeated.

"I think so," said Roland at last.

Jess stood up.

"I *knew* it," she exclaimed. "I mean, I could feel him. Look, I'm going home. I want to think about what to do next. But I'll ring you."

"Right," Roland said. "Sorry if I've made things complicated, but—"

Jess interrupted him. "It's not your fault," she said. "You didn't know. And anyway, you've found yourself, so you'll never be one of the lost ones—not now. Of course, finding yourself might be the death of you," she added, and laughed.

"Oh, well, as long as there's something to look forward to," said Roland, sounding much more like his usual self. And he stood too, looking briefly at Jess and then past her toward the lions in their glass case. Four pairs of yellow eyes met his.

"Hey!" he cried.

In spite of her anxiety Jess laughed again. "You've caught on at last!" she said. "But you need to be quicker than that."

The lion and the lioness were standing where they had always stood; the cubs were playing as they had always played. But they were no longer looking at one another. They were all staring at Roland himself.

SUNDAY

Jess and Roland met the next afternoon and spent it all (or so it seemed to Roland) talking and walking through a country that, though he knew it well, was, for a day at least, a landscape of dreams. Up in the hills beyond the city they scrambled along rocky tracks. When they met other weekend scramblers, they fell silent, and then when they were alone once more, they went on, as if they were old friends meeting after being parted for a long time.

"You can't shut it out. So open up to it!" said Jess, sounding like a school counselor or a tennis coach.

But something's wrong, Roland was thinking. *She's not like she was last Saturday. She's not even as sure of herself as she was yesterday. And she looks used up in some way. Used up and discarded!* All the same, he was trying to do what she told him to do. There on the hills, when Jess turned her face to the sky, he relaxed, lifted his own face, and welcomed the wave that moved toward him and engulfed him—the wave that was not just one sound, but a host of sounds; not just one sensation, but a multitude—letting it sing through him as a single force.

"When I think about it," Jess was saying slowly, "when I *think* about it and don't just—you know—*live* with it, it seems as if light is growing deeper and deeper around me. Deeper and deeper without getting any darker. But I've lived with it a long time now, and I don't notice it unless I make myself think about it. It's just there—always there. It's what I am."

"But doesn't it push in on everything else?" he asked. "I mean, we've got to breathe ourselves and cut school lunches, oh, and piss, too, and work on assignments and fight with our brothers and all that. I know now I've been able to hear bits of it for years, but there's always been this voice warning me. 'Careful! Careful!' it says, making me step back."

"What voice?" asked Jess.

"I don't know . . . just a warning voice inside my head," Roland replied. "But I haven't heard it for a day or two. It must have given up on me."

"It's been different for me from the way it's been for you," said Jess. "Being at school and all that has been like real life for you, hasn't it, but it's been like camouflage for me. In the beginning I came to school like a lot of little kids do, thinking I was so wonderful that people would see my wonder and like me for it. But of course they didn't. I mean, they didn't *mind* me, but they didn't take any true notice of me, and they still don't, as long as I do reasonably well (but not *too* well) and don't rock any boats. I'm not pretty or good at sports or anything distracting like that, but I'm not bad at things either. So I just cruise along looking dim—oh, but not *too* dim, because there are some teachers with ideals who might try helping me if they thought I was slow, and I don't want help. I come home, slam the door behind me, and just sink into it—into the color or the sound or whatever you want to call it. I go back into my own head, I suppose . . . back into my own cells and further back, until the stuff of the world makes way for me and I can go in every direction."

As she spoke her eyes, which had been fixed on his face, did their trick of contracting, then opening again. Her whole face was flooded by a transfiguring happiness. "It's just so . . . ," she began, and then broke off and gestured as if there were no words to describe what she was talking about, and she must use an ancient sign language instead. But indeed Roland, the smart man with words, already knew that what they were experiencing together was beyond language.

"Okay, but outside life *is* real," he objected as much to himself as Jess. "Just as real, anyway. More real!" he added, and saw her frown. Now when he looked at Jess, he found he was seeing not the roughness of her hair, or the vanishing pimple above her left temple, but her long eyelashes and her beautiful lips. "You can't say it's more real in the heart of an atom on its own than it is when the atoms join together to make something," he argued. "A book or a flower or ice cream. Anything!"

"No," Jess agreed. "But we're sort of programmed to take no notice of most things. I mean, we don't look deeply at dust or dead leaves because—well, there's no human *profit* in looking at them. There's no space and time for that sort of looking, and we can't deal with the distraction of it. We just vacuum the dust and dead leaves up and throw them away. Yet, if we looked . . . *if* we thought . . . every grain of dust is a universe. That's part of what is singing to you right now. And not only that, no one ever asks us in chemistry textbooks what being an atom *feels* like. And when you find out, it's like understanding a poem—only more than that. It's like actually *being* the poem."

Suddenly she leaped from the path onto one of the great rocks thrusting out through the thin soil of the hills and ran out along the rock to stand, arms flung wide.

"Watch out!" yelled Roland, sure he was going to see her slip and tumble away into the void below, wheeling just as she had wheeled in his vision, but toward death this time. However, she stopped right on the pouting lip of the rock, arms still raised, and shouted into the air:

To see a World in a grain of sand,
And a Heaven in a wild flower,
Hold Infinity in the palm of your hand,
And Eternity in an hour.

"An ho-o-ur!" she shouted, howling like a woman with wolf blood, and the hills howled back, "Ho-o-ur! Ho-o-ur!" Roland felt every one of his hairs writhe against his scalp, each with an agitated life if its own. Jess wheeled on the very edge of the rock, arms still raised, lips still parted. Then she let her arms fall to her side and laughed.

"William Blake!" she called back to him. ("Blake . . . ake . . . ake!" the hills cried in chorus.) "I think he was like us. He saw visions. He knew, didn't he? He must have. To write that!"

Recovering from his shock of fear on her behalf, Roland looked at Jess as if she herself were a vision. She had terrified him, and yet he could not remember ever being so thrilled in his life before.

"Oh, wow!" he exclaimed. "It sounds as if you've really opted out of everyday life, and you're putting all your energy into this other scene." He tore his gaze away from her, glancing from side to side and trying to treat the sticks and stones around him with tolerant dismissal. But they would never be dismissed again. He would live smudged into them for the rest of his life.

The city below signaled to them as light caught on windows of houses and cars. Beyond the city lay the plains, embroidered with the erratic silver of rivers, while beyond the plains rose the mountains, lightly dusted with the first autumn snow. The ski slopes weren't open yet, but they soon would be. Roland wondered if this was not an inappropriately worldly thought at that particular moment.

"It's all part of the same thing," said Jess, walking back along the rock toward him, and Roland realized that in some way she had caught his unspoken thoughts and was reassuring him that skiing still had its place. Behind and below her one particular long city street, lined with autumn trees, caught the light and shone out like a wand of gold.

"What about Hudson?" asked Jess almost shyly.

"What about him?"

"What will you do about it? Make something up? It wouldn't work. You might fool Hudson, but Quando would know. He's good at knowing. He can read people's minds, and he can shift things without making his nose bleed. . . ." She broke off. Roland saw yesterday's uneasiness and apprehension take her over once more.

"What's wrong?" he asked.

"Nothing," Jess said, and then, realizing that he would not

believe her, added, "Well, something *is* bothering me a bit, but I don't want to talk about it right now. It's so great walking around up here and just . . . just *being.* So, what will you do about Hudson?"

Roland shrugged.

"What's the worst that can happen?" he asked. "They won't expel me. Not for a first offense."

"But if he goes to Mr. McDonald, he might make it sound worse than it was."

"It *is* bothering me a bit, but I don't want to talk about that," said Roland, mimicking her. "You're right. Let's forget troubles and concentrate on *being.*" They strolled on, Jess going ahead, Roland following her. "I've got a plan," he called.

"What plan?" she demanded.

"If you're so clever, you should be able to read it out of me," Roland replied.

"I don't do that," she said. "And besides . . ." Fear, or the memory of fear, briefly haunted her voice.

"But Quando listens in, doesn't he?" asked Roland. "You told me he collects other people's power."

"He can rip it out," she said, making a snatching gesture to emphasize her words. "Out and away! He's so desperate to be the strongest one that it's turned him into a vampire. Not a blood drinker, but someone who feeds on intuitions, like ours. And whatever he eats—however much he eats—it's never enough. Never! It only makes him hungrier. And his feeding destroys the source." Jess took a deep breath. "Once he tried stealing *my* power. He knows . . . that is, he *knew* my parents a while ago. And in the beginning I liked him. He told me jokes. He was playful and did all sorts of tricks—well, you probably know the sorts of things he does. One evening, though, when we were walking home together through the Riverlaw Reserve—he'd just been voted into Parliament back then—he offered to *share* with me. Well, he called it sharing."

"Share?" asked Roland. Jess walked steadily on, though the path had suddenly become steep, and treacherous with small, slippery stones.

"I was a bit lonely then," she said severely. "I was happy to try sharing. I said okay." She came to a sudden stop and turned to him. They stood face-to-face, high on the hillside in a tangling wind that was snatching the words from her lips. "But he didn't want to share. He just wanted a way *into* me. He wanted to . . . to *feed.* It was rape—a sort of rape," she exclaimed. Then, before Roland's eyes, though he could not say quite how, Jess altered. She became frightening. "Well, it *might* have been rape, but I was too strong for him. Too strong, too strong!" she added, almost singing the words. "The trouble is, it's only made him determined to . . . to *have* me, if he can, and right now (not that I want to go into all that) I mightn't be strong enough to hold him off."

Roland decided not to question her about the things she was not telling him. There would be time to wonder about them later. And later still, he thought, she would let him know.

"I reckon Quando somehow locked on to me and *nudged* me into shoplifting," he said, "so that Hudson could blackmail me into getting to know you."

"Could be," said Jess. "They probably thought you'd be able to . . . to lever the door open so that Quando could slide in as well."

"But it's not just to do with you. It's something to do with your parents, isn't it?" Roland asked, and saw the anxiety she was so unwilling to share with him possess her once more. "Isn't it?" he persisted. "Hudson asks about them, particularly your mother."

"Just leave it!" said Jess rather sadly. "Don't even ask! It'll work itself out. What *you* should be worrying about is Quando. Because, as I said, Quando wants it all. He'll want you, too, and you're so new to things he might actually *get* you. And there's no recovery. You'd bleed forever."

Roland considered this. He found he believed it. If that sea-sound of change were to be ripped away from him, he would indeed bleed forever, withering as he bled. A changed man, he looked at Jess, then past her to stare into the sky above the city once more. Color and sound melted into each other.

"Listen, I'm thirsty," he said at last. "If I take you to my house, my mum and my brothers will spy on us. Let's go to *your* place. You do make a good cup of coffee."

Roland was still looking into the sky as he said this, but he felt her shrink, as distinctly as if he had seen her do it.

"So, what's wrong?" he asked, still looking into the sky, yet knowing just what expression she was wearing.

"Nothing's wrong," she said stiffly.

"What? You just want to be alone again," he mocked. "Hey, look! I know you're lying."

"Well, they're *my* lies," she said. "I don't have to share them. I'll hold them in front of my face and peep around them. You think of *your* troubles and I'll think of mine. Concentrate on what you're going to do about Hudson."

"Oh, that!" Roland said airily. "I've already worked out what to do about that. By this time tomorrow it'll be all over and done with, and I'll bet that's more than you can say for all your troubles."

CONFESSING

"Did you have a good weekend?" asked Chris. She was friendly enough, though not as friendly as she would have sounded a week ago. As she stood there before him with the light on her beautiful hair, and her slightly tilted eyes dark against her pale skin, Roland suddenly understood how certain warm lifts and falls in Chris's voice, along with the happy tumult of her words, had once tied them together. He half wanted to offer her an apology, because the least he owed her was some anguish at losing her, but at that moment he couldn't think or feel about Chris in any urgent way. Jess! Jess Ferret! In spite of her moment of ecstasy on the rock yesterday, he knew something was dangerously wrong for Jess. It was her business, of course (he mustn't intrude or try to force her to tell him anything she wanted to keep to herself), yet whether she acknowledged it or not, he was already part of her struggle.

"I did ring you," he told Chris a little defensively, and heard his voice betraying lack of interest and sounding increasingly guilty because of that betrayal. He had plans for the day ahead, about which he had spoken to no one, not even to Jess (after all, if she was allowed to have secrets, so was he). And while he was saying this, he actually *saw* Jess, walking across the playground on her own toward her usual tree, and caught himself staring at her across Chris's shoulder as if she were the only thing worth looking at. "You were out," he said.

"I went out with Stephen," Chris said. "I didn't want to sit at home just waiting around for you to ring me in your own good time."

"It wasn't like that," Roland began, but the words tumbling into the air between them had no real conviction. Jess was opening her book as if she was planning to read, and he wondered if she was merely pretending to read and was really linking into that tree. The diagrams of last year's biology suddenly sprang into his mind—she might ride, he supposed, through the long cells that carried water from root to leaf. She might sit at the growing tips of the tree feeling the explosion as cells divided. Or, of course, she might do none of these things. He was simply imagining what she might do if she felt like it.

". . . but there wasn't much on," Chris was saying. "Once autumn comes, everything closes down."

"Sure does," agreed Roland, nodding absently. His real life would never be here on the seats under the school library windows again. Everything had narrowed to Jess Ferret sitting in solitude under the linden tree.

"That's what I mean," he heard Chris saying as if from a distance, and broke out of his trance to find her looking at him almost contemptuously.

"Sorry," he said. "I was dreaming."

"All you've dreamed about this week is Weaselly-Ferret," said Chris. She sounded as if she could hardly credit what she was saying, but was saying it anyway. "You're always staring at her. Do you think I'm too dumb to notice? Why don't you go over and talk to *her* instead of sitting here pretending to be interested in me?"

"I'm not," said Roland. "It's just . . . I mean, last week we were talking about a book she was reading, and I was just wondering if she'd finished it—that's all."

But he knew, as he spoke, that Chris would never believe his stumbling excuses.

"She just carts books around to make herself look interesting," said Chris. "If you think she actually reads them, you're even dumber than she is." For the first time he could remember, she sounded actively spiteful.

Stephen came toward them and sat down confidently on Chris's other side.

"It was terrific, wasn't it?" he said. "I keep remembering it."

"What was?" asked Roland, a little sourly.

"Didn't you tell him?" Stephen asked, unable to keep triumph out of his voice. "We went to this rave at the Caribou. Quantum Leap were playing," he added impressively. "It cost a packet, but man, was it *worth* it!"

"Was it worth it?" Roland asked Chris, feeling the ghost of a resentment that really belonged to that earlier self. Then he gave her a faint grin that was almost conspiratorial, but which only seemed to infuriate her.

"Not that you'd care," she said crisply, leaping to her feet. "I'm off! No need for you to bother yourself."

"Actually, I've got to go too," said Roland, looking at his watch. "I've got to check with old McDonald about something."

"You in trouble?" asked Stephen, standing up and moving in beside Chris so that *they* were the pair and Roland was the odd man out.

"Hope not," said Roland.

Chris and Stephen turned away, but then, unexpectedly, Chris turned back.

"Are you really okay?" she asked in rather a different voice. "Really?"

"I'm great. Just great!" said Roland as lightly as he could, and her expression became both petulant and puzzled.

"Oh, well then! See you around!" she said sarcastically, and she and Stephen walked away together.

Going, going, gone, thought Roland, watching them retreat with a sort of nostalgia for a simple past self, rather than with true regret at losing Chris. *Gone. No way back.* Then he, too, turned, walking off in a totally different direction, sighing and wincing as he made for the nearest door to the principal's office. Mr. McDonald, no doubt restored by lunch and cups of tea, should be in his room by now.

He was. Five minutes later Roland was standing before him, confessing to his shoplifting and looking as repentant as he possibly could.

Mr. McDonald listened, staring at him expressionlessly. His head was small and bullet shaped, and the eyes behind his glasses, though slightly clouded, behaved rather like bullets too. Roland felt their twin regard strike into him over and over again.

"What a mean little crime," Mr. McDonald remarked at last, his voice mild yet ringing, Roland thought, with a mixture of contempt and curiosity. "It doesn't seem like your sort of thing at all."

Mr. McDonald did not sound in the least tolerant or forgiving, yet Roland felt an unexpected relief. It was only what he had thought himself, over and over again.

"I don't know, sir," he said, shaking his head, trying to mime the exact bewilderment he had felt this time last week.

In the end all he could do was meet Mr. McDonald's gaze blankly. "I really don't know."

"Not knowing is no excuse," exclaimed Mr. McDonald, sounding a little disappointed, almost as if he had expected a scholarship student of Crichton Academy to come up with something much more impressive by way of an apology.

"I've got the things here," Roland said, "and I'm going to take them in after school . . . not just to put them back," he went on hurriedly. "I'm going to tell someone what I've done. Confess! Get clear of it."

"Well, you've done the right thing coming to me," said Mr. McDonald, and Roland could already tell from his expression that he might provisionally be forgiven. "I'm interested that you've bothered to tell me about it," he went on in the judicial voice of a principal commending a sensible decision. "Why did you?" he added curiously. "Conscience?"

Roland played with the idea of telling Mr. McDonald that he was trying to anticipate the reaction of a blackmailing teacher, but decided against making life any more complicated than it already was.

"I thought that when I told people at the supermarket what I'd done, someone might ring up and let you know about it. I thought I'd better tell you first." It sounded reasonable enough. He could certainly see it making sense to Mr. McDonald.

"Well," said the principal slowly, "I suppose this latter-day honesty is better than nothing. Of course, it was a serious lapse on your part, and don't think I feel at all easygoing about it. On the other hand, I don't expect people to be perfect even if they do happen to be senior students. Go to the supermarket and make your confession. Tell them to get in touch with me if they want to. And then let me know tomorrow how it went. In the meanwhile, I'll think about what I should do about it. If anything," he added.

Halfway there, thought Roland, walking through the corridors of the school, filled with relief by now rather than shame. He'd finished with shame. All the things that had worried him a week ago—the possible disgrace of being struck off as a prefect, as well as the thought of having to confess to his mother—were still alive in him, but the wish to escape from the Hudson trap was overwhelming. Halfway there! It was even possible to feel cheerful. The thought of pouring out a confession to Mr. McDonald had frightened him in quite a different way from the prospect of talking to a supermarket supervisor. For Mr. McDonald knew him, knew his friends and family, and had the power to disgrace him publicly in a personal way. The worst was behind him.

Later in the afternoon he found he had underestimated the humiliation of a supermarket confession. Having first raced home to change out of his school uniform, and having dutifully chained his bicycle in the rack closest to the supermarket, Roland refused so much as to glance through the window of the blue-and-silver café, in case he met the ginger gaze of Quando, but strode past it and in under the lighted arch of the mall. Ignoring plastic baskets and shopping carts alike, he plunged into the heart of the bright maze of islands and aisles. Rather uncertainly, he approached a girl in a blue smock who was refilling a shelf and asked if he could speak to a supervisor, half supposing she would lead him to a private office somewhere. However, she hurried over to the delicatessen section to stand subserviently behind a man in a long blue jacket. He was talking earnestly to the woman behind the counter, bending forward as he did so, tapping on the glass of the display case and pointing at the sliced pork in a significant way. When he finally turned toward the girl at his elbow, apparently irritated by her interruption, she pointed at Roland, and he stared briefly at him, a faint, impersonal smile flicking across his face as he did so.

At last the supervisor turned and came briskly toward Roland. Halfway across the intervening space a flash of startled recognition, then puzzlement, and finally something much more forbidding, crossed his face. *He can't* know, thought Roland with sudden dismay. *Oh, damn! He does! He does!*

There seemed to be a mutual understanding that what they had to say to each other must be said in private, and they automatically moved away from the girl replenishing and straightening the shelves so that she would not hear them.

"Well, how can I *help* you?" the supervisor asked, emphasizing the word *help* in a way that suggested its opposite. Already scarlet with embarrassment, Roland began his tale of theft and pillage, but as he told his shameful story a woman with a shopping cart approached, and the supervisor drew him still farther into the maze so that his confession was finally completed beside a castle of brightly colored plastic buckets. At last Roland fell silent and, without looking directly at the supervisor, dipped into the plastic bag he had been carrying to produce the pens and the notebook, together with money for the pie, setting them out neatly on the base of a green bucket. The man picked up first the pens and then the notebook, turning them over, apparently searching for any sign of damage.

"I actually knew about you," he said unexpectedly. "We've

got you on video. Shoplifting is a huge problem for us, and there are cameras. . . ." He broke off, glancing up toward a corner of the high ceiling, then peered at Roland, hoping, perhaps, for some evidence that he was impressed by this sophistication. Roland had nothing to say, and the man gave a brisk little sigh before he went on. "No one was actually watching the screen at the time you pulled off *your* little tricks. But I always check the tapes late in the afternoon, just to get an idea of anyone we should be watching out for, and I certainly remember you." On and on he went, speaking with weary irritation, about the meanness of shoplifting, pointing out that it added to the price of things, which made life harder for old-age pensioners and people on welfare, and generally lecturing Roland as if he were a five-year-old. Roland listened, nodding penitently, punctuating the lecture every so often by saying, "I'm sorry! Yes, I know. I'm sorry!" (*I'm in real trouble this time,* he was secretly thinking.) But having talked his way through his irritation, the supervisor suddenly relaxed.

"Look! I'm prepared to let it go this time," he said, "since you've owned up and brought the stuff back."

Had Roland been pushed into shoplifting because Quando the Magician had slyly entered his head by some back door and nudged him into it? But even if he *had* been nudged, he now knew he had welcomed that nudging. Somewhere along the line—just when, he could not say—he had grown inwardly dissatisfied, *bored* with his own labored excellence, bored with himself as the good son, and bored, too, with that inner voice saying, *Careful! Careful!* all the time. Sometime, somewhere, he would have to sit down and think about this. Sometime, somewhere, he would work it all out. But not now, not now, for he was in the supermarket, and the supervisor had talked himself in a circle and was repeating his first complaints. Yet, oddly enough, the supervisor was not so much reprimanding Roland as confiding in him. It was as if Roland's confession had somehow united them in mutual understanding, and though the supervisor was still frowning, his expression somehow suggested that *he* was the confused one.

"I don't know how people can do it!" he exclaimed. "God knows we bring prices down as low as we can." Then, abruptly, he seemed to remember that he was speaking to an active, if repentant, criminal. "Don't think I'm being soft," he said, shaking the packet of pens at Roland like a reproving finger. "If you set foot in here again, I'll be watching you, right?"

"Right!" agreed Roland with fervent sincerity. The man gave him a chilly smile, then turned sharply and walked off, carrying the pens, the notebook, and the money. A few minutes later Roland was unlocking his bike and making for home.

He had not really pictured himself being clapped in a prison cell. All the same, he was surprised at the new sense of space around him. Both Mr. McDonald and the supervisor had been disarmed by his confessions. There were no humiliating results so far—not public ones, anyway. His outer excellence was intact. He was still a prefect, and he was free. Honesty had proved to be the best policy. Worn out by public repentance, yet light and airy, too, Roland cycled home.

Suddenly, for some reason, he knew that someone was looking at him. He felt the impact of this regard fall like a hand on his shoulder. And he knew, still further, that whoever had recognized him was continuing to watch him. Over the past two days he had occasionally felt glances brushing across him like insubstantial hands, but on this occasion the contact was a clutching one. A familiar blue car drew alongside him and slowed down a little. Mr. Hudson was driving past, glancing sideways, looking ahead, then glancing sideways once more, just as Roland himself had done when tracking Jess more than a week ago. Their eyes met, and Mr. Hudson gestured with a stabbing, urgent finger to a parking space several cars ahead of them. Roland had anticipated this encounter but had thought it would not take place until school the following day. All the same, he found that, in spite of his weariness, he was almost glad of it. *Get everything over and done with all at once,* he thought, pulling his bike in beside the sidewalk. And he was happy that the encounter would not be at school. Out here, free of the Crichton school uniform, he would be his own man again. No! He would be a *new* man, and ready to go on to the next thing.

Mr. Hudson, having parked his car in the empty space, leaped onto the sidewalk and came to meet him, working his eyebrows as if they needed urgent exercise.

"Missed you after school," he said heartily, his eyes flickering over Roland, checking him out for still more stolen property, perhaps.

"I didn't have anything else to tell you," said Roland. "It's been a busy weekend."

"You didn't see Jess at all, then?" asked Mr. Hudson, that avid expression shamelessly dominating his face. He made no effort to dismiss it. It clung there—an unabashed declaration of self-interest. Here, out of the classroom, on the edge of a city street, with traffic moving steadily past them, things were almost open between them.

"No, I didn't see Jess," said Roland. "And I didn't see her mother, either. I was too busy . . . sir," he added, open insolence creeping into his voice. Why not? He, too, could be unabashed if the situation justified it. He saw his tone register with his teacher. But something else—something much more urgent than mere lack of respect—was distracting Mr. Hudson.

"You're lying," he exclaimed. "You spent time together on Saturday and then again on Sunday."

"Are you keeping a watch on her too?" Roland asked incredulously. "Then, what do you need me for?"

"I'm *worried* about her," said Mr. Hudson. This assertion sounded more like an automatic mantra than like something he really expected Roland to believe.

"Why?" asked Roland challengingly, speaking as if to an equal. "She seems fine. And anyhow, I don't want to spy on her anymore," he said. "Sir," he added, amazed how rapidly a traditional respect was turning into its opposite. There was a brief silence.

"Look at me!" said Mr. Hudson abruptly and in a totally different voice from any Roland had heard him use before. Strong in his new power, Roland looked at Mr. Hudson directly, and Mr. Hudson fell back a step, his expression changing.

"By God," he exclaimed, "that bitch has taken you over."

In spite of his confidence, Roland was astounded, for Mr. Hudson—the teacher he had known for three years—was altering before his very eyes. Face-to-face with a savage stranger, he felt his own expression changing to one of shock and bafflement.

"Yes! Go on! Stare! Pretend you don't know what I'm talking about," hissed Mr. Hudson. "Do you think I can't read it in you?

I might not be one of the *chosen* myself," he said with a dreadful bitterness, barely moving his lips as he spoke. "I might have been excluded from the company of *gifted* ones, but I can recognize the gift in other people. After all, I've lived eye to eye with it all my life. Oh, don't worry! I've been reminded over and over again that I've been passed over. But why you?" asked Mr. Hudson venomously. "Why bloody *you*?" Then he spun around, made for his car, scrambled in, slammed the door, and within half a minute had edged out into the flow of traffic and disappeared.

Roland watched the blue car for as long as he could. Then he climbed onto his bike again and made for home, while the roar of the traffic and the other outer music of the living city wove themselves together to sing in his ears, and not only in his ears, but right through him. He biked on, feeling that, at any moment, the thin boundary of his skin might disappear and that, transformed into a single, urgent note, he would ring out over the suburbs and then higher and higher until he dissolved somewhere among the stars. A weed growing through a crack in the sealing of the road spoke in a green voice. The fenced-in trees spaced out along the pavement, a piece of wastepaper driven by a slight breeze to throw itself under the wheels of his bike, all sang to him in their different voices. The contrary world quickened, faded, and quickened again. *I'm happy,* thought Roland, taking it all in, amazed by the quality of his acceptance. *I feel happy.* Which was as close as he could get to naming what it was he really felt. Pedaling on, he turned the word over and over in his mind, making it a question (*Happy? Happy?*), followed by an exclamation (*Happy!*).

But then from somewhere under that feeling, or perhaps even from the heart of it, a voice cried for help. Roland's bemused smile vanished. He listened keenly without hearing that cry again, but his exalted mood was lost and gone. Turning in at the gate, he slowed, dragging his foot along the ground to bring the bike to a standstill.

The cry came again . . . a cry of weariness and despair. He recognized not Jess's actual voice, but the quality of Jess—the *taste* of Jess. It was unmistakable. Now he found he had been planning, almost without being aware of it, to call in on her later that evening—to call in and somehow to talk her into surrendering her last mysteries to him. Making up his mind, he turned his bicycle once more, pointing it toward the road.

"Where are you going?" yelled Danny from the porch steps.

"Mind your own business," he called back.

"Chris! Are you going to see Chris?" called Martin, preparing to make fun of him.

"Yes! Tell Mum I've gone to see Chris," he cried, and began pedaling down the drive, making for the street that led to the avenue that linked up with the main road, which would take him back to the illuminated temple of the mall, to the Riverlaw Reserve, and, finally, to Jess's green door.

"'Childe Roland to the dark tower came,'" he muttered to himself, and this time it was more than a private joke. It seemed as if it might be a true command.

THE DARK TOWER

Once again Roland came through the narrow alley; once again he jogged out onto that green strip of grass below tattered autumn willows. Once again he turned toward Jess's house.

"The door's locked," said a voice. Roland came to a standstill and looked sideways, though he already knew who was talking to him. Quando was sitting on one of the park benches, staring toward the green door too.

"She wouldn't let *you* in anyway," he said to Quando. Quando turned toward him, narrowing his eyes, almost as if Roland were too bright to be looked at directly.

"Oh, I've no doubt she would open the door to you," said Quando. "She would if she could, that is. But you see, she can't! That house has closed in on her. It's crushing her to death. No one will be able to go through that door until she is dead."

He seemed strangely formal in his black town coat. The big shopping bag at his feet made him look as if he was trying to disguise himself as a tired shopper taking time off in the middle of a spending spree, and his expression, as he looked at Roland, was difficult to read, though Roland could certainly hear a revengeful pleasure in his voice. Shut out on the wrong side of that green door, Quando was longing for disaster to fall on Jess. Perhaps he hoped she was dying and that, as she died, he might perform the vampire act of which she had accused him . . . perhaps he hoped that he might still somehow manage to break into her house, to bend over Jess as she died, breathing in her last breath as she breathed it out, taking final possession of her powers.

It occurred to Roland that this was the first time he had seen Quando's face free of white paint or shadows or the distortions of an odd angle of vision. He was a rather handsome man in a slightly overweight way, but the ghost of the same anger that had filled Mr. Hudson a little earlier was now haunting his brother.

"I'd keep well clear if I were you," he said, shifting restlessly. "I really would." As he shifted light fell on him from a different angle, and now Roland was able to see—to see clearly—something that had escaped him at first glance. Though he was struggling to hide it (to hide it even from himself), Quando was afraid. "Don't go near the place," said Quando.

"Well, you just sit there," Roland said. "Or shoot into the café and have a glass of wine. I'm going to find Jess."

"You'll never do it," said Quando. Roland wondered if the sound of Jess's weeping was filling Quando's head the way it was now filling his. A chill that had nothing to do with autumn was seeping across the river and attempting to enfold him in an implacable embrace. He must move on. Striding down the slope and over the footbridge, he felt himself gasping as he struggled to ignore the panic rising within him. He ran up between the neat hedges, almost flinging himself toward the green door, lifted the Medusa head, and knocked loudly.

No one answered. For all that, Roland could feel Jess somewhere beyond that door. She was in there, weeping, and not only weeping, but tormented. Had Quando been able to feel that torment too? From between his fingers the brass Medusa, its enormous teeth bared, grinned at him.

"You can't frighten *me,*" Roland muttered, twisting the handle beside it, only to find that, sure enough, the door was locked. *Open,* he thought at the door, wrenching at it, trying to rattle it free of its lock, but it was a desperate command with no expectation of any obedient response. Yet his head was immediately filled with the song of iron. A fluctuating image began to form, springing into existence apparently in answer to his command. Suddenly he was seeing a lock . . . the mechanism of a lock . . . this very lock, perhaps. There it was again, a diagram behind his eyes. While he focused on it, frowning in confusion, iron and steel sang at him and through him. Then the image was gone.

Roland paused, closed his eyes, and tried to order it back once more, feeling like a clumsy child attempting to use a pen for the first time. Slowly the picture of the lock reformed, drawing its shape from the resonant song of iron as well as from the actual lock in front of him. It vanished once more and then, at his repeated command, reformed for a third time. "Don't move! Don't change!" Roland cried, daring it to disobey. "Freeze!" Struggling to hold the picture inside his head, he put out his hand to give force and guidance to another, interior hand, which he now felt himself extending toward the image. No! It didn't work. Try again. He reached out a second time, both outwardly and inwardly. Outwardly and inwardly he touched the lock. Inwardly he gave it an experimental nudge, and in the outside world he heard a click, as if a key had turned. *I'm doing it,* thought Roland. *I'm nudging the world.* He opened his eyes and touched the door handle hesitantly, as if it might suddenly have become red hot, then gripped and turned it. Very slowly the door swung open.

Grinning with incredulous relief, he pushed it wider, expecting to surprise late-afternoon light along the hall, but as he looked into Jess's house his grin grew fixed and then was wiped away by something close to horror.

For he was confronted by a narrow, twisting darkness, though *darkness* was too familiar and friendly a word for that savage absence of anything, that negation, that chaos shot through with continual tremors of pale light. Somehow Roland immediately knew that those streaks of light had nothing to do with any season or time of day in the outer world. Like the lines in geometry that have extension but no width at all, these persistent, bleaching lines were hinges on which the ordinary existence of things was swinging and failing. Recoiling, he stepped away, stumbled, and almost fell backward down the steps. Faint yet clear, from a park bench on the other side of the river, he heard mocking applause.

Roland regained his balance, more by luck than judgment. Taking a deep breath, he straightened out of the half crouch into which he had automatically fallen, and wriggled his shoulders (which were hunched forward as if expecting blows to fall across them) into a more formidable line. Somewhere from the heart of this chaos Jess Ferret was calling for him. It must be for him. There was no one else for her to call. Something (he didn't dare to guess what) had gone terribly wrong for her. Still, Roland hesitated, staring into the banded darkness beyond the green door. A sensible man would have waited on the opposite riverbank, as Quando was waiting. A sensible man would have slammed that door and walked—no, run. A sensible man would have run and run, screaming as he ran. No one would blame him. And yet he, Roland Fairfield, was not going to behave like a sensible man. He was going to step *through* that door and into that dreadful trembling chaos, even if it meant that his own reality might falter and fail. *No choice,* he told himself firmly. *Don't try working it out, just* do *it.* Perhaps by inheriting his father's role, perhaps in some ways by *becoming* his father, he had been practicing for such a moment—the moment when he would face something from which his father had always turned away. *Here I am,* he made himself think. *I'm alive. I can think. I'm doing well at school. I can work things out. Okay, so it's terrifying. So what! Hearing your mother cry night after night—that's even more terrifying, and I've lived through that. I've even almost made it up to her. And that was real. And I'm real too. Not really perfect, of course, but perfectly real.* Then he kicked the door wide open and stepped through.

CLIMBING WITH CLOSED EYES

He could not see an inch beyond his nose. Squinting down in its general direction, he found he could not even see his nose. All the same, still whistling and hissing to himself, reminding himself how real he was, then nodding and muttering agreement with himself, Roland stepped forward yet again, before pausing and groping backward. The door handle seemed to thrust itself gratefully into his palm. He closed the door firmly behind him, shutting everything safe and familiar away on its other side. Shutting Quando away too. Then, just in case he should find himself tempted to make a run for it, he pulled the picture of the lock back into his mind. It came much more readily this time (he must be learning that particular trick of command), and nudging it with his thoughts once more, he heard the lock in the outside world click home. No retreat! No retreat! He had locked Quando out and himself in.

Roland had stepped into an alien state. The fog that now closed in on him was not really a fog, but something insubstantial and nameless, the negation of everything that had sung to him as he cycled home only a little while before. It wrapped itself, layer on layer, around him, and here in this terrible house—this house that was more than a house—he found it easy to believe that the true world, maddened beyond all sense, was savaging itself, devouring itself, then vomiting itself back as this peculiar, striped absence of anything. It might be an insolent illusion, perhaps, or then again, perhaps not. He struggled against it, stepping forward, blinking and gasping as he did so, unable to hold any sort of real picture of the stairs or the kitchen door. The picture ledge, which he knew was running around the walls of the hall a little above head height, was quite invisible, and so was the silent company of coats, hanging in rigid folds above the pairs of boots, which someone in the past had lined up neatly beneath them. All the same, the spaces around him rang with sound. It came at him from every direction—the sound of someone lamenting.

"Jess!" he called, though he did not really expect an answer, and indeed there was none, though the pitch of the lament seemed to change—to become, somehow, more despairing, more ferocious.

Roland closed his eyes. He struggled to remember the exact shape of the hall, and, miraculously, its image came into his mind so quickly and precisely that it was as if he were actually seeing it. The detail and conviction of this image took him aback so severely that he was startled into opening his eyes once more, whereupon the undulating, streaked confusion rushed in on him with the malevolence of a nightmare. Shutting his eyes again, Roland stepped hesitantly forward into the spaces with which his memory was presenting him. Putting out his hand, he groped for the handrail of the remembered stairs. Miraculously, smooth, rounded wood seemed to rise up under his fingers. "Good dog!" he said aloud, patting it and laughing a little. Relaxing, too, he felt immediately that his laughter had done something to relieve the anguish of the house. Lifting one foot, he found himself secure on the first step of the stairs. He risked opening his eyes once more.

Anarchy was still raging around him, but he thought he was now able to see *through* it—that he could almost make out the rising line of the stairs and the angle at which it met the landing above. Then, looking upward, he found he was suddenly far from alone. A whole company of tenuous figures was moving down toward him. *Ghosts,* he thought, unable to think of any other word for this succession of advancing, opaque figures. Those closest to him had faces in which there was no single, reliable feature, for his active vision melted everything it fell on. Mouths dissolved. Eyes bubbled and liquefied. There was nothing that could be looked at for as much as a second, let alone be recognized. Farther up, toward the top of the stairs he made out faces that resisted any change at all, faces that stared like the faces in old photographs, fixed forever in some past moment. Most of them were faces he did not know, but even as he considered this he saw someone he felt was vaguely familiar . . . someone he thought he had occasionally seen at school. Jess's mother, perhaps! Yes! It had to be Jess's mother, which meant the man behind her must surely be Jess's father. And there came Jess herself—many Jesses—a hopeful, plain child of about three, a cautious child of eight, a ten-year-old saddened by her own apartness, a girl of thirteen able now to rejoice in solitude, all of them stepping down the stairs toward him, all holding firm at first, then seething and disintegrating.

The ghosts descended toward him, only to fade and disappear before reforming at the top of the stairs. And among this volatile throng, unmoving this time, stood the creature, looking down at him with an expression Roland was unable to define. He couldn't call it wicked or malign, and yet, looking up at it, he felt something shift uneasily low in his belly and believed, with horror of quite a different kind, that his bowels were about to turn treacherous on him. He'd read of people shitting themselves in moments of fear.

"Oh, come on, Childe Roland!" he cried aloud. "Forget it! I don't even know where the bog is in this house." And he quickly shut his eyes once more, stepping upward boldly. What he couldn't see might not be able to hurt him.

"Go on! Tell them," he ordered himself, reminded now of the old line that seemed to have been written for him. "Let them know who's coming! 'Childe Roland to the dark tower came,'" he shouted aloud for the second time within the hour, and the sound of his voice caused the staircase to reform itself behind his lowered lids, empty and almost normal, except that now he saw the rising steps more vividly than anything else he had ever seen in memory. Details he could never have known declared themselves. Worn edges to the carpet on the stairs first made themselves visible and then were felt underfoot. They were not speculation or dream, but were re-creating themselves at his command. That weeping was clearer now—the only sound he could hear. It seemed to fill the whole house, and more than the house. The sound of that weeping filled the world.

Eyes still closed, Roland stepped up a third step and then a fourth, certain now that he was walking safely upward against the flow of ghosts. He began counting.

". . . ten, eleven, twelve . . ." Then he paused again.

"Jess!" he called. "I'm coming." He kept on climbing (. . . nineteen, twenty . . .). At his next step he almost toppled, and believed he was going to tumble into nothingness before he realized that he had safely reached the landing. There was no higher step for his feet to find. So far so good!

Then he hesitated, trailing his fingers experimentally across a section of wall. After all, he had never been in this part of the house before. The image, forming obediently behind his closed eyes, insisted that there were doors in front of him, and that the nearest door was the one through which he must go. Roland walked toward it, putting his hand unerringly upon its handle, which he turned just as he had turned the handle of the front door. Both seen and unseen, the door opened easily, and as it did so his inner sight darkened. Perhaps, thought Roland, it might be because his inner sight was no longer needed.

So, cautiously, he opened his eyes a little, determined to face anything that might be prepared to show itself.

SPELLS

Once again he was confronted by annihilation. But this time there was a break in it . . . a peephole. There was a patch directly in front of him where the incoherence failed, and there, coiled tightly in a chair, her knees drawn up to her chest, her arms hugging her knees, was Jess Ferret. She was the source of the disorder. The sound of her weeping came to meet him.

"Jess!" cried Roland, aware that it might be the first time he had ever called her by her name. She raised her head to look vaguely in his direction but said nothing.

"What's happening?" he asked her.

"I'm falling to bits," cried Jess, uncoiling and leaping from her chair. Standing before him, weeping and trembling, she did indeed look as if she might be about to disintegrate.

"No way!" Roland cried, stepping forward and catching one of her frantic hands in both of his. It struggled in his grip like some animal desperate to escape. Then, not knowing how else to reassure her or himself, he pulled her, clumsily, into his arms. At first it seemed he was grasping at nothing more than a colored shadow with no more shape or substance than a northwest wind. But then he tightened his grip and gradually felt her growing solid and constant once more, felt her pressing against him and weeping on his shoulder.

"I'm sorry," she was crying, "I thought I had everything—you know—under control. I thought I'd be able to put myself together again and wake them when I wanted to. I thought I'd win. But that's the trouble," wept Jess. "You think you've cracked it . . . you think you're in charge of it all. But you aren't! Everything's disconnecting, and I'm disconnecting too."

"Fight it," said Roland. He could not understand what she was telling him, but words, no matter how ragged and incomprehensible, were better than nothing. "I'll fight with you."

"But it's all my fault," Jess cried, pressing herself desperately against him. "I lost my temper and went too far, and now I can't go back again. I've lost my power."

But Roland was suddenly feeling an entirely different confusion, though one he recognized only too well. Sexual desire swept through him in waves of hot compulsion. He kissed the corner of Jess's mouth, then kissed her again, full on her lips this time. Jess's lips moved under his as she tried to go on with her incoherent explanation, but he kissed her again. She was still for a moment, as if she were making up her mind about a new taste. Then, slowly, she began to kiss him back.

"Oh," she murmured when the kissing ended, and they paused to breathe. "Oh, gosh!" (like a little kid impressed by some magician's trick).

Desire cast a spell of its own. The incoherence seemed to be losing its domination and falling away from them. A room began to take shape around them. Figures began to emerge, slowly growing more precise and detailed with every second.

It was, in its way, a sumptuous room, dominated by a huge double bed draped with a quilt of a crimson so deep that it looked almost black except where the curves of its gathers and folds caught the light and smoldered, as if they were about to break out in flames. To his left stood a chest of drawers whose triple mirrors reflected a silver hairbrush and a silver powder bowl and not one, but three vases of flowers, arranged as if for a funeral. Indeed, Roland thought they might be artificial, until the mixed fragrance of roses and lilies hit him like a soft, scented blow.

It was not just the flowers that made the room funereal, however. Lying side by side on the bed were two people who appeared to have been laid out for burial. The woman's hair was gray at her temples, and there were fine lines around her closed eyes. Soft creases ran from nose to mouth. Still, she was a good-looking woman even in what Roland quickly understood to be a state of unnatural sleep. He knew at once who she must be. He had seen her ghost on the stairs only a short time earlier, along with the ghost of her companion—a man with thinning, faded, fair hair and a craggy face as pleasant as any face could be in such strange circumstances.

"Are they dead?" Roland asked.

"No," Jess answered. "They're under a spell."

This room did not have the arrested feeling of the kitchen, fixed forever in a single moment and rejecting change. It now seemed to be struggling to keep dissolution from taking it over once more. The door flapped a little. Beyond it Roland could still make out the seething incoherence through which he had climbed, and imagined it taking over once more. Still, the room's details seemed to be safely restored as far as he could tell. He looked from the hairbrush and the powder bowl to a picture on the wall. Jess, framed in silver, looked shyly back at him. There was a broom just inside the door, its handle tilted back against the wall, its head guarding a small heap of gritty dust, which had obviously been there for a while. The floor had certainly not been swept recently; it was thinly carpeted with dust. He could see his own footprints marching between the door and Jess's chair. He looked back at Jess, and they kissed each other again.

"Now?" said Jess breathlessly.

"Not now," Roland replied. "The bed's full and the door's so flirty."

"What?" cried Jess, her voice still shaking. She looked toward the door and the flickering existence beyond it.

"Come on! I'm talking your language," Roland said.

"What?" Jess repeated blankly. Then suddenly she laughed, and as she did so the tension around them eased. Perhaps laughter confronted chaos, and by matching it, somehow contained it. Roland shifted his gaze to the man and the woman, side by side on the bed.

The man and the woman were not dead. They were both breathing—both smiling slightly. Roland believed he could see shadows moving, not across but *under* their eyelids . . . the movement of their dreams, perhaps. They were lying to attention even in their sleep, feet placed neatly together, hands straight at their sides, and even in their smiling trance they both seemed to be concentrating on something—perhaps on those shadows shifting under their lids.

"Roland," Jess said. "Roland?"

He had spoken her name, and now she had spoken his. The room became even more certain of its own existence.

"It's me," he replied. "What's going on?"

"I thought I could hold it all together," she said. "I was so thrilled with myself in the beginning—sort of guilty, but excited, too. You know! But then it all got away from me, and I can't put it right again because I've—well, I've *damaged* myself."

"How?" Roland asked, and then as she hesitated, "And what about them on the bed! Your mum and dad! What's happened to them?"

"I shouted 'Sleep!' at them," she replied stiffly. "I *ordered* them to sleep and they slept."

"I'd better be careful," said Roland, "or you might put a spell on me. Of course, maybe you already have," he added. Jess shook her head.

"No," she said. "I'll never do that again. I mightn't be able to, even if I wanted to." Then she began to cry in a rather snuffling fashion. "Never! Never! Never!" she said. "'What I tell you three times is true.'" Then, once again, she laughed, though tears were running down her cheeks. "Have you ever read *The Hunting of the Snark*?"

"Yes! That's what we need right now. A good discussion about books!" exclaimed Roland. He felt his fear retreat still further. "Right on! But I could do with a cup of that coffee first. Let's make for the kitchen."

"Coffee?" exclaimed Jess incredulously. "You've come all the way up those stairs and through all those ghosts to order *coffee*?"

"Or tea," he said. "Or some sort of ordinary life. When we believe in it hard enough, we make it happen."

"You go," Jess said distractedly. "You make it. Tea or coffee . . . whatever you like! Then bring a cup up to me. I don't think I'll ever go downstairs again."

"Oh, come on! Don't be a wimp!" Roland exclaimed. "I mean, I got up here, didn't I? If I can get up, well, you can get down."

"You *kissed* me," Jess said, as if she had only just realized it. "Didn't you? Do it again." Roland obeyed, and this time Jess kissed him back with desperate, confused kisses, so that it seemed as if her inner chaos were flowing out through her lips and in between his.

"All this is crazy . . . too crazy," Jess said, breaking away from him at last. "I mean, Sleeping Beauty and the prince didn't behave like this, did they? He gave her one kiss and she woke up, rubbed her eyes—"

"And probably said, 'Hey, what's for breakfast? Tea or coffee?'" said Roland. "Listen!" he went on, shaking her gently. "If you put a spell on your parents, why don't you take it off? Take it off now."

"I can't," she replied. "I've tried and tried. But nothing works. Because, as I told you, the force of the spell . . . it sort of . . . it disconnected *me.* I've turned into my own ghost. And I'm frightened. More than frightened."

"Do what I'm doing," advised Roland. "Take a deep breath." Her breasts moved against him as she followed his instruction. "Now! Let's make for the stairs. I'll count. One . . . two . . ."

He kicked the door wide. They looked into collapsing space. Jess gave a panicky cry.

Down the Stairs

"No, no! It's all right," said Roland quickly. "Take it from me, everything's coming back. Shut your eyes and remember it the way it was—because that's the way it really *is.* If you stumble, I'll catch you. And you do the same for me. Let's go!" He stepped onto the landing, not looking at it too closely, taking his own advice and treating the material world as if it were safely there, waiting to welcome him. Floorboards took form under his feet. "Come on," he said, drawing her after him. "Don't be fooled by all this. Just keep your eyes shut."

Step by step, Roland leading, they groped their way across the landing and began to walk down the stairs.

"I've opened my eyes," said Jess, speaking in a much more controlled voice. "You're right. It *is* coming back."

"Believe a bit harder," he urged her.

"Did *you* see the ghosts?" she asked unexpectedly.

"Yes," he said. "Most of them were you at different ages."

"Most of them were people who have lived in this house," she said. "It *remembers* them. They're part of its hidden—I don't know—its hidden *texture,* and when I cast my spell, the house's memory turned them loose. They—"

"Don't think about them," Roland cried. "Not yet. Look! Here we are at the bottom of the stairs. And there's the kitchen door. And while I think about it, just to take your mind off things: Tell me, why are there so many flowers in this house? Vases and vases of them. Are you taking lessons in flower arrangement or something?"

Jess laughed. It was almost her usual laugh.

"You and your gang all call me Weaselly," she said. "But my name—the Ferret part of it—actually comes from an old Italian word, *fiore,* which means 'flowers.' I hate the name Weaselly—I just *hate* it so much, even if I pretend not to mind. So, here at home, I've been trying to remind myself over and over again of my true meanings."

"Ferret! Flower!" said Roland. "In a funny way it suits you. It really does. Okay, here's the kitchen. Tell you what—you sit down, and I'll be mother. Lord! It's only six thirty. It feels like midnight. Midnight last week."

Thinking back to the first time they had sat together in this kitchen, Roland found he remembered exactly where things were kept. He chattered about nothing as he filled the hot-water jug and then located cups and coffee, and as he did so the rigid state of the house continued to yield. He had not wakened a Sleeping Beauty when he kissed Jess (after all, she had been awake already), but perhaps when she kissed him back, her kisses had set something free both within her and in the house, too. He could feel it slowly escaping not only from chaos, but also from its own previous immobility, and working its way back to being a simple house once more.

Roland peered into the lit cave of the refrigerator. It was almost empty, but he found a bottle half filled with milk.

"I do feel changed," Jess exclaimed behind him, not sounding exalted in any way, but pleased and puzzled.

"Me, too," said Roland. "Not just feel, either. I *am* changed. No going back."

He poured water onto the coffee. He felt himself leaving fingerprints on the handle of the jug and on the coffeemaker—fingerprints that were being accepted. They would stay there until someone rinsed and dried the jug and the coffeemaker, washing them away.

"You wouldn't think kissing would make so much difference," said Jess wonderingly. "I mean, it was special to me, it truly was," she added quickly, "but it's an ordinary thing for people to do, isn't it?"

"I don't know why either," said Roland. He put the coffeepot down in front of her. "Does that look as if it will be okay in about five minutes?"

"Yeah, fine!" said Jess absently. "Mind you, kissing is supposed to break spells."

"It's supposed to cast them too," said Roland. "And now you'd better give me some clue about what's been going on. I deserve to know by now, don't I? So tell me."

JESS'S STORY

Jess sighed. "It's hard to know where to begin," she said. Then she stopped to laugh again. "There are a lot of times when storytellers say they don't know how to begin, but they're actually beginning by saying it."

"Maybe there aren't any beginnings," suggested Roland.

"Hey, wouldn't old Hudson love *that,*" said Jess. "Scholarship stuff! Top marks!"

"*Begin!*" Roland commanded her. "Tell me all! Now!"

"Well, in a way all this"—Jess waved a hand around her—"started because my father and I—but I told you about that the other day. And I told you about Mum and Dad making the house over to me and taking it in turns to visit me here, which was fine. Until about three months ago, that is, when Mum suddenly got serious about someone—Tyrone Hudson. Not that I *minded* too much," Jess cried quickly, before Roland had time to say anything. "And anyhow, in the beginning I thought I liked Tyrone—until I saw he'd, well, he'd *collected* from my mother. She didn't seem to mind, but then she'd never been held by . . . by *alchemy* in the way that Dad and I were. You, too, just in case you haven't caught on to it yet. But Mum wasn't like us, and Tyrone's different again. I don't think he's curious about the *greatness* of things out there. I think it scares him. But he does want to be the big boss of everything. In charge! So he steals the energy out of other people and feeds it into himself. Well, I've told you what he tried to do to me. Of course, my mother just wouldn't believe Tyrone was any threat to me. I know she told my father I was *insecure.*"

For no reason he could be sure of, this misunderstanding seemed to be a link with the uneasiness Roland himself experienced at times with his own mother. Family life seemed full of dangerous negotiations.

"Mum really believed," Jess continued, absorbed by her own story and unaware of Roland's speculations, "that if she was kind and understanding and patient, I'd eventually come round. And my dad thought I was being a traditional difficult teenager."

"That seems a bit weird," Roland said. "Wouldn't he understand through . . . through the connections of alchemy?"

"Yes, but right then he didn't *want* to understand," said Jess, "because he had plans of his own. My parents treated me like a grown-up, which seems great, but it was partly because they were longing for me actually to *be* grown up. Then they'd be free from me and from each other, too. Not that any of us had really worked it out like that. Anyhow, about a fortnight ago Mum and Dad turned up together saying they had something serious to talk about, and that we were all reasonable people with our own points of view, and that we'd talk it through. Blah, blah, blah!"

"I know that sort of discussion," said Roland, grinning. "Go on!"

"They were getting a divorce," Jess cried. "My mother wanted to marry Tyrone, and my father wanted to go traveling. He said he'd put it off for years because he didn't want to leave Mum on her own, looking after me, without some sort of support. But now . . ." She looked down at her clasped hands.

"Sounds pretty reasonable," Roland said, speaking cautiously, however, for he already knew that it had not seemed reasonable to Jess—not reasonable at all.

"But don't you see? They'd fooled me! And I'd *fooled* myself," Jess cried passionately, glaring down the table at him. "All that feeling of being in charge of my own life! All that business of being trusted and mature and so on. *A* for *apple,* I wasn't trustworthy. And *B* for *bloody bummer,* they'd been tricking me by more or less telling me I was. Because once my dad was overseas, things were going to change. Tyrone was a member of Parliament, and he lived in Wellington a lot of the time. So my mother was moving to Wellington too, and of course I was going to have to go with her. I was going to have to leave this house—*my* house—because once my dad was gone, it would be a totally different scene. And this time they were really hanging tough. I mean, they *did* try to be sensitive about it all, but every so often their faces just lit up with their own secret delights. And then it turned out the discussion was a sham anyway. Dad had already booked his flight. I think they had been a bit . . . well, *scared,* which is why they put off telling me until things couldn't be changed. I don't know. I just don't know. Anyhow, we had this huge fight. And at one point I . . . I hated them . . . *hated* them. And love and hate are like energy, particularly for people like you and me. And the hate turned into a spell. It just sprang out of me."

She looked defiantly at Roland, who looked back at her, trying to find useful words. But now Jess was caught up in her own story. She raced on frantically.

"My parents—well, you saw them up there. I suddenly had total power over them. I marched them up the stairs and I laid them out as if they were dead. 'That'll teach them,' I thought. But then I found that I'd—well, I'd damaged myself. Damaged the house, too."

"It froze," said Roland.

"If you like," she agreed.

"Right," said Roland. "So that's why Quando has been stalking around on the riverbank staring at your door. He was there again tonight. Did you know?"

"Tyrone!" Jess sighed. "Is he? I would have known once, but I'm just not sure about things in the way I used to be. I do know that for the first day or two he was away in Wellington being a member of Parliament. When he phoned, I told him to leave us alone and mind his own business. Big mistake! But what else could I say? And I was sure I could defend the house against him."

"I expect that's when he and Mr. Hudson honed in on me," said Roland. "They needed a sort of lever and thought I'd do. In the beginning Hudson kept on asking sly questions about whether or not I'd seen your mother. But hey—didn't you feel the least bit *worried* about your mum and dad frozen up there?"

"Well, in the beginning I did feel a bit guilty, of course," Jess admitted, "because though I hated them for about ten seconds back then, I really do love them—both of them. But I felt . . . oh, triumphant as well. It was just so thrilling—being defiant, I mean, and winning out over them all. I was . . ." She made a face. "I was exalted."

Roland remembered standing at her doorway last Saturday—it now seemed an incalculable time ago. He remembered her radiance had amazed him.

"It shone out of you," he said.

"And, of course, I thought that I'd be able to snap the spell whenever I wanted to," Jess said. "I imagined them recovering and being humble and doing things *my* way. But then I found my true power had broken free of me and was stalking around like a ghost. Oh, I could still play a bit—turn the gaze of lions and so on—but that was all. Really, I was torn in two and haunting myself."

"That ghost! What did you call it? The thingummy! The

eiderdown?" said Roland, getting the name wrong on purpose. He wanted to make Jess laugh, which she did.

"Eidolon!" she exclaimed. "The *eidolon*! Get it right! Look! It's me . . . part of me. I've reached out to it . . . called to it . . . commanded it. I've tried to . . . to embrace it. Nothing's worked. It walked through you, but it won't walk through *me.* And over the last day or two I've felt myself shrinking. And the house—my *home*—has turned frightening around me."

"I'll tell you this," said Roland. "Whatever was going on over here frightened Quando/Tyrone. He spoke to me on the riverbank, but he was too scared to come any closer." As he said this Roland felt his own words immediately begin to nag him.

"He'd know something was happening, I suppose," said Jess. "He knows and he nudges. That's probably why he's so up-and-coming as a politician."

"Mind you, *I* nudged the front door," said Roland. "I unlocked it with my nudging. So I'm one up on Quando, because I'm not out there shivering on the riverbank, am I? I'm here with you."

They looked wonderingly at each other, as if in spite of sitting in the same classrooms for years and years, as if in spite of their jokes and desperate kissing, they had only just been introduced.

"How do you do?" Jess said unexpectedly, smiling and holding out her hand.

"How do you do?" Roland replied, gravely taking her hand and shaking it formally. "Great to meet you." As he did this he understood what it was that had bothered him only a moment ago. "Listen!" he said urgently. "The house may be haunted by the eidolon, but it isn't frozen in the way it used to be, is it?

Won't Quando be able to *feel* that? I mean, mightn't he be able to—to get in?"

Jess abruptly sat up straight.

"Maybe," she said doubtfully. Her expression changed. "I mean, probably he will," she exclaimed, starting to her feet.

At that moment there came a knocking at the front door.

A Hook in the Head

The knock was not loud. It was almost shy. All the same, it was threatening. Roland and Jess both knew that whoever was waiting on the other side of the door was not a friend or neighbor or some earnest caller hoping to pass on an evangelical magazine.

The knocking came again. Now it was demanding. Roland pushed the kitchen door open, and he and Jess stood, side by side, staring down the hall.

Silence. Then a faint clicking sound. They could not see the door handle, but they could hear it twist, squeaking minutely as it did so.

"Insects from another planet," whispered Roland, doing his best to joke, for even as he froze with apprehension, laughter seemed to have power.

"Did you lock it when you came in?" Jess asked.

"Yes," said Roland. He could remember the soft, conspiratorial sound the lock had made, turning and clicking even though there was no human hand on it.

Abruptly the wood around the lock of the green door exploded inward, splintering wildly as it did so. The door swung open, banging violently against the wall.

Quando seemed to fill the doorway. The black silhouette of his head against the outside light of the Riverlaw Reserve reminded Roland of Mr. Hudson's head, a shape that he had seen over and over again, silhouetted against the big chalkboard that dominated the English classroom. Uninvited, Quando stepped over the threshold and came stalking along the hall of Jess's house toward them. Behind him came Mr. Hudson, but slinking, not stalking.

"Oh, good evening, sir," said Roland, talking to Mr. Hudson, using his best Crichton Academy voice overlaid with all the sarcasm he could muster. Mr. Hudson did not reply. He did not have time to do so, for Quando began talking so loudly and confidently that anything his brother might have to say would have been drowned out anyway.

"I've been patient," he said. "Patient enough! I'm getting tired of waiting. Roland—that's your name, isn't it? You may have come into your power, but I doubt if you can marshal it sufficiently well to cause me much trouble. And Jess! Admit it! You're down and out. I was a little nervous about calling on you until about twenty minutes ago, but suddenly there was no longer anything to keep me at bay. So you're both going to have to bargain with me, after all, or I promise you, things will become extremely unpleasant. Though you do seem to be recovering. . . ." He stopped, staring at them. "Oh, I see!" he said, sounding unpleasantly amused. "You've been wasting your energy playing love games."

Though he had been determined to stand firm, Roland found himself retreating back through the kitchen, Jess beside him, as Quando advanced.

"Life will be simpler and better for both of you if you are

set free of it all," he declared, "and I am here to set you free. Besides, you don't deserve your powers, you know," he added, shutting the kitchen door behind him, and very nearly closing it on Mr. Hudson.

"Get out!" yelled Jess. "Just get out and leave me alone."

"You heard her!" cried Roland. "Get out!"

But Quando took another step forward, and they retreated yet another step, while Mr. Hudson glared at them from the shadow of his brother, his eyebrows contracting in a frown, then arching once more.

"Of course, nature squanders her riches," said Quando. "Some people are recipients of the talent when they don't know what to do with it. Fools who dream of stars, for example, and cowards who refuse to accept what is being offered."

"Or greedy collectors, like you," cried Jess breathlessly, "wanting to play games with people's lives."

"Yes, I do want to play games, and big games too," Quando said. "Better games than people can play themselves. Jess, your mother never used *her* power for anything but play. And what do you ever do with yours? Listen in to plants and stones? Eavesdrop on worms? Pass it on to me, and climb into bed with the boy here. I swear you won't miss it after a day or two."

"And do I deserve to lose my power?" Roland asked.

Quando shrugged. "You're about to be relieved of it anyway," he said. "Make it easy for yourself. No struggling! No petty attempts at revenge! Because that would irritate me, and I can't bear irritation. Do remember that if I have to force it out of you, it could be painful."

As he spoke his ginger brown eyes slid around the kitchen, flicking at the coffeepot, the sink, then lingering on the book spines. Finally he fixed his eyes on Jess once more.

"Oh, I see," he said, looking annoyed. "It's not *in* you. Have you tried hiding it away from me? But it'll have to come out of hiding when I pronounce my own particular abracadabra."

"Get out!" cried Jess again, drawing herself up as if she were planning to strike him.

Quando flung his right hand over his eyes as he raised his left-hand palm outward.

"Don't try it!" he cried. "Don't try it. I'm warning you."

Roland had the impression that even though Jess had lost much of her power, Quando was still afraid of her. If so, the magician recovered quickly.

Something happened—something Roland could not quite define. The clear air seemed to writhe . . . a movement like two pieces of flawed glass being swung across each other. Jess stumbled. Then she was lifted off her feet and hurled violently against the wall under the bookcase. She fell in a heap on the floor and did not move.

"Tyrone . . . ," exclaimed Mr. Hudson.

"Oh, I *am* sorry!" said Quando. "I overdid it a little, didn't I?" His voice became a little boastful. "When one's strong, it's easy to forget just how strong one is."

Roland was shouting as he rushed at Quando himself. Then the space in the kitchen warped and stretched, and Roland found himself tilted helplessly forward, gripped in an invisible vice. Quando smiled at him from what seemed like a great distance.

"Don't waste your time being *brave,*" he said, his voice coming and going, now far off, now blaring discordantly as if his lips were next to Roland's ear. "Think yourself lucky I don't smash you against the wall as well. I've tried being patient. I've tried being kind. I have even played with the idea of possible partnership, but neither of you has chosen to cooperate. Well, I shall just *ravish* it out of you—out of *both* of you, my dears. It will hurt. I'm sorry about that, but that pain passes. You'll recover, I promise."

But Roland, shutting his eyes against Quando's smile, understood that his new dimension had become part of what he was. There would be no recovery from that loss. Still, in order to fight back, he had to know what was going on. He opened his eyes again.

The kitchen was restored to its usual dimensions. Roland found himself crouching but unable to move. Jess lay, partly propped against the wall, looking stunned and entirely helpless.

Careful! said a familiar voice in Roland's head. That inner voice, that voice that had prompted him year after year and that had fallen silent over the last two days, was talking to him again. *Watch out!* it said, speaking with a new urgency. Roland took a breath and then . . .

Then he was engulfed in pain. An invisible hook struck down through his skull, its tip exploding into the brain below. Roland found his mouth stretching impossibly wide, though the sounds he longed to make could not force their way out of him. He writhed on the floor. From somewhere behind him Jess began screaming.

"It's what I *am*. It's *me*!" she yelled in a distorted voice at Quando. "You're destroying me."

The strange thing was that Quando was also groaning as if

the effort of entering them, of locating and commandeering whatever power they had, was hurting him.

"Tyrone," said Mr. Hudson, stepping forward. "For God's sake, Tyrone, do be careful. If they were to die . . . if you were to kill them . . . Oh, God! Be careful."

But Quando, still groaning, struck Mr. Hudson across the chest, and Mr. Hudson fell back as if he, too, were being clubbed and torn.

"Come to me," groaned Quando. "Oh! Oh! I'm calling you. Be mine. Be *me*!"

The kitchen door opened. Jess's parents stood framed in the darkness of the hall behind them. Their eyes were open, but Roland could dimly see, through his cloud of anguish, that they were still wearing the exact expressions they had worn lying side by side on the crimson bed upstairs—the same slight, secret smiles. Quando rolled his eyes toward them, a ghastly smile twisting his face.

"My dear," he cried to Jess's mother. "There you are! But it's not you I want to see right now."

The tormenting tug went on. Struggling against it, Roland rose to his knees but could get no farther.

"Where is it?" screamed Quando. "What have you done with it?"

And at last a third shape appeared in the doorway. The creature—the eidolon itself, wavering and semitransparent—stood there, staring at them.

"Oh, yes!" gasped Quando. "Oh, yes, I see. I see!" His eyes rolled toward Jess. "I'm going to swallow all that matters of you. The boy can have what's left."

"Tyrone! Don't!" cried Mr. Hudson.

"Please!" wailed Jess.

But the eidolon was all that Quando desired. He was turning away from them all. He was flinging his arms wide. "Walk through *me*!" he cried.

The creature wavered like a reflection on windblown water. It took a step toward him. Its face shifted and flared like a beacon. Roland knew that if it tried to walk through Quando, it would never emerge again. Jess's parents stood there, still and smiling, utterly dominated by Jess's enforcing spell.

"Yes! Yes!" cried Quando, arms still wide.

The creature moved confidently toward him.

Oh, fabuloso! said Roland's inner voice.

A point of light formed inside Roland's head. It began between his eyes and ran through his veins and arteries, navigating the chambers of his heart like burning blood. Abruptly he found he was free to move again, and that though he had fallen to the floor as one man, he was rising as two.

"Stop!" he cried. The voice that came from between his lips was not his own. It was someone else's voice—a long-ago voice speaking out of memory. In the middle of her fear and torment Jess rolled her head to look at him, while Mr. Hudson frowned in his direction, as if he could not recognize his familiar pupil.

"Here I am," Roland heard himself shouting in this new voice. "Home again! Deal with *me.*"

Quando was straining forward to urge Jess's eidolon into him. But something about the voice coming out of Roland broke into even Quando's longing. His arms fell to his sides; the creature stood still. Unwillingly, Quando turned to look at Roland.

"We're too strong for you," said Roland's inner voice,

speaking as an outer voice now, its words leaping—yes—from the springboard of his tongue and out into the kitchen. He had no idea what was going to emerge from his mouth until he heard the words coming back into him through his own ears.

"Too strong for me? You and who?" asked Quando, forgetting Jess—even forgetting the eidolon—looking back at Roland with a threatening expression that was also nonplussed. But then he broke off. His expression changed. "*What* are you?" he cried. "Where did *you* come from?"

"It's me," said Roland, struggling to speak for himself. "Me and . . ." He paused. Two stick figures walked side by side through his head—separate people, but smudged together along an inner boundary. "Me and my father!" he shouted in amazement.

"Your father!" yelled Quando. "He's gone. You said he had gone."

"He's with me now," Roland said, and knew it was true. Wherever his father might be in the world beyond the city, he was also there in Jess Ferret's kitchen, bringing with him whatever strange talents he had been punished for revealing in his childhood—powers that he had denied but that had built in strength, day after day, year after year. As they flared through Roland he felt himself growing strong once more.

"Trickery!" said Roland, speaking in his father's voice, then saying it again—("Trickery!")—in his own. "There's more than one sort of trickery. You see, my father had to trick his mother, and to do that he had to trick himself. I had to trick myself," he found himself crying aloud in that other voice. "I wouldn't let myself believe what I truly was. I betrayed myself, so in the end I betrayed everything and everyone I loved. There was nothing left of him," said Roland, speaking with his own voice now, understanding more and more of his lost father and speaking both for him and with him. "Words lost their meaning. Love froze in him. He fled," said Roland, telling his father's story not only to Quando, but also to himself. "He's never left me. He's always been alive in me. He's talked to me. He's warned me. And now he's here. I'm here. He's coming—I'm coming—into his, into my, own." And Roland laughed, astonished to find he was making something that was almost a pun.

Quando stared at him, taken aback by his laughter as much as anything else.

"You may be more than I thought you were . . . ," he began, sounding uncertain, and perhaps even a little frightened.

"Why, we could eat you alive," said the voice coming out of Roland's mouth. "It's been in us for years, flowing between parent and child, parent and child. Now you see it. Now you don't. We are the *true* magicians."

And then, Roland, being only himself now, danced around in front of Quando, mocking him, while all sorts of shifts and alterations took place behind his eyes. "Free at last!" he shouted in his father's voice, "Free at last!" he shouted in his own. "Let's all be free." And he flung out his arm, pointing, making in the outside world a gesture he felt his father making inside his head. Behind Quando, Jess's parents suddenly blinked, turned their own heads, and looked at each other with dazzled bewilderment, while Jess slowly picked herself up, staring all the time at Roland.

"You lay in my coffin!" Quando cried to him. "Remember my power." There was something almost pleading in his voice by now.

"Feel mine!" said Roland in his own voice. He had no idea what he was going to do next. He simply flung out his arms as if he were going to fly.

The room fell away from him. He was suspended in space. Once again he could see those bright grains, not still as they had been when he first saw them, but moving in a design of light. And there was his mother, with his brothers circling her. There he could just make out Jess's parents spinning face-to-face, while beside him he could see a stranger he already knew—a different version of himself. He and his father spun together, staring into each other's eyes, until, slowly, he became aware of Quando, no longer a man about to take flight, but someone suspended in the first instant of an endless fall. He beat around wildly, twisting his head from side to side. He yelled; he screamed and writhed. He wore an expression of mortal terror.

"Be still!" Roland called to him. "It's in the stillness." But Quando could not hear him. He certainly could not hold still.

A line—similar to a line in geometry, length but no dimension—twisted in the space beside them. In a sort of reverse dissolving, grain by grain, the eidolon took form and, ignoring the tormented Quando, drifted toward Roland.

"Not me!" Roland cried as it advanced. "You don't belong to me."

He looked for Jess, wondering whether, since she had had the essence of herself torn away, she had been unable to reach this other space—this space where everything became fulfilled by simple existence.

But then he saw her just as he had seen her when he lay in the wonder box, in Quando's coffin of visions, for the second time. There she came, spinning toward him like a wheel of fire. Once it had frightened him. This time he watched her come, knowing they must collide. He held his arms wide open.

It was as if the creature moved through him again. He closed his eyes, opened them, and found himself standing in Jess's kitchen with Jess in his arms.

Something had altered. It was as if some piece of a jigsaw puzzle that had never quite fitted suddenly slid easily into place. Holding her tightly, he looked over her shoulder. Mr. Hudson was pressing himself shakily against the door. Quando lay facedown on the floor. Both of Jess's parents were standing in their earlier places, but they were people once more, not dolls. They were looking at their hands, turning them over, and incredulously studying first their knuckles and then their palms. They touched their own cheeks, ran their hands over their hair, then felt their own forehead before turning to each other in bewilderment. The eidolon was gone. And Roland's father—that old inner voice, the part of himself that (he now understood) had always been his father trying to protect him from his own strangeness—had retreated. All the same, there was a fulfilled presence in his head. What had been a detached voice had become a flowing connection.

Roland turned to find himself looking directly into Jess's unexpectedly blue eyes and immediately knew she was whole again. Her mother exclaimed. Jess released him and turned as her parents moved toward her, and they clung to one another with confused forgiveness.

On the floor Quando turned over. He seemed like a different man.

"What happened?" he asked, and his voice sounded piping

and childish. Suddenly he screamed. "Who am I? Who am I?"

"Tyrone!" said Mr. Hudson, falling on his knees beside his brother. "Tyrone, what's wrong?" He looked at Roland with mixed fear and accusation. "What have you done to him?"

"I don't know," said Roland. "The same thing he was going to do to me, I suppose," he added.

"Something's *happened* to me," wailed Quando.

"You've ruined him . . . ruined him," cried Mr. Hudson.

"Take him home. Put him to bed," said Roland, trying to sound kind, though deep down he felt nothing but triumphant.

"I'm not what I was," wailed Quando. "Where's it gone? Give it back. It's *mine.* It's *me.* Give me back to myself!"

Fabuloso! said an unrepentant voice in Roland's ringing head.

A CALL FROM BEYOND

Roland got off his bike and stared up at the sky. He did not know much about the stars, but he could see that Orion was sinking in the west, while in the east the great Scorpius was rising. His feet seemed to be barely brushing the ground, and he felt that he was both here and there, crossing the lawn to his own back door and simultaneously suspended between the constellations.

The world around him was echoing and curiously spacious—even empty—yet its very emptiness seemed richer than all its usual crowding. He thought of his father. He thought of Jess and her restored and bewildered parents. He remembered how he had helped Mr. Hudson support Quando as they passed the neat hedges, crossed the footbridge, and scrambled along the alley to Mr. Hudson's car. Roland came to understand that Mr. Hudson was deeply fond of his younger brother, and that while he was furious at Quando's defeat, deep down he was feeling something like triumphant relief, too. Quando, the bright bully, must now depend on him for a while. "He *will* get better," Roland had said to Mr. Hudson. "Well, I think he will. He hasn't had it torn out of him . . . not like Jess."

"Shut up!" said Mr. Hudson. "Just shut up."

"Did he inherit it?" Roland had asked. He couldn't help asking. "Was your mother or father able to . . . Or did he learn it? Or steal it?"

But Mr. Hudson did not reply.

"What's happened to me?" Quando was asking yet again in that newly childish voice as Mr. Hudson slammed the car door, then drove off into the night.

What had happened to Roland himself? He understood something by now. Both his father and grandfather had had that extra sense, but various things—the times they were living in, and Roland's puritanical grandmother, of course, along with her stern views of what should be decently possible in a puzzling world—had made both of them shrink from becoming wider selves. For all that, they had found furtive fulfillments. His grandfather had planted a garden in his daughter-in-law's dreams, and his father had seeded Roland with something of his own identity and had lived a branching, secondary life in Roland's head. Lost as he was in the world out there, he had still tried to care for Roland, had been able to feel his transformation, and had been able, in the moment of crisis, to bend the space that separated them and to strengthen him with the forces developed during his solitary wanderings. Roland understood that since his father had left his family so ruthlessly, he had had time and space to move through ancient restrictions and prohibitions and had won himself a strength of his own. Jess, divided, had been weakened. Roland, reinforced, had become strong.

In the doorway of Jess's house Roland had kicked the fringe of the long carpet, glad that this time it would stay disordered. Jess's house now felt as his own home did, as all family houses did, a natural sphere of disorder. He and Jess hugged each other, but gently this time. *Hey! Tenderness!* thought Roland. *It's not very trendy, but I'm good at it. I must have had secret practice.* And oddly enough, he caught himself remembering once again how, years and years ago, he would wake in the night to hear his mother weeping softly as she fed the baby Martin.

"I'd stay with you," he said to Jess. "Well, I *will* stay if you want me to. Only it seems as if you have to do the next bit on your own."

"I know," she said. "Mum and Dad—they need help to find the world again. They need to find themselves, too, because everything's changed. And . . . and . . ." She yawned hugely. "And I want to sleep until Christmas. New Year, even! New Year, you near!" she added, and laughed.

"How about waking up tomorrow?" suggested Roland. "Or the day after? Soon it'll be the weekend. Pity to miss that. Besides, we've both got assignments to do. I'll bet old Hudson marks me down. Okay! I'm off. There's just one thing. I want to say it. I know you know what it is, but I want to hear what it sounds like in the outside air."

"Say it, then," Jess said.

"I love you," he said. "I know I do."

Then he had cycled home, so exhausted he could barely push on the pedals, yet feeling free . . . feeling pure. All his dislocations and confusions had fallen into place, then disappeared. No doubt there were times when they would sweep into him again, but tonight, at least, his other self, his sleeping magician, had been recognized and had had a chance to speak and reveal itself. Over the next few days—over the next few years—he would have to work out a way of slotting it in with all the rest, but that could wait. Biking home through the city night, he had been at ease with the world. As he put his bike away he could hear his mother's voice trembling as she shouted, presumably at his brothers. Roland grinned. Family life! The shouting ceased as he crossed the yard.

He leaped up the steps and opened the door to walk into his own house, then came to a sudden stop. He was home. This was *his* house, not Jess's. Yet, though every single thing in front of him was totally familiar, it felt . . . it felt *unexpected.* The shouting had stopped, and so, it seemed, had everything else. It was quiet. Usually as he stepped through that door he would *hear* things—would hear his mother clattering dishes and telling Danny, for example, to behave himself, while Danny yelled back, thumping the wall and sticking up for himself by blaming Martin for something. Usually he would smell food.

But tonight Roland was being greeted by something strange and intense. His mother was talking, but she was talking almost breathlessly, holding the receiver of the phone as if it were a newly discovered and delicate wand. Only a few minutes earlier the room had rung with cries of furious amazement—somehow, he could still hear those cries, although by now they were nothing more than the echoes of echoes. Danny and Martin were not so much sitting as crouching by the heater, both mouths a little open, yet both contained by rare, total silence.

"Yes! Yes, of course!" Roland heard his mother say in that strange, quiet voice, perfectly calm yet somehow charged with feeling. How could such ordinary words sound as if they meant everything? Her voice was a little hoarse, roughened by her earlier shouting.

As Roland stood in the doorway his brothers' eyes turned toward him, round with excitement, but then immediately swung back to their mother. Neither of them said a word.

"Yes," Mrs. Fairfield was saying. "Yes. All right. Soon. Well, the sooner the better." She laughed a little. Tears rolled down her cheeks as she laughed. Yet the feelings Roland sensed in her were not feelings of sadness, but rather of violent confusion and, marrying into that confusion and slowly beginning to dominate it, relief, as if a long-endured pain was fading at last. "All right! We'll look forward to it. What? Oh, yes, he's just this moment come in. No, I won't promise anything either. We'll just see how we go. Bye, then! Good-bye!" She was finishing a conversation she did not want to finish. "Good-bye until . . . Good-bye!"

She put down the phone, turned toward Danny and Martin, opening her mouth to speak, then glanced toward Roland instead.

"What is it?" asked Roland, while his brothers continued to stare at their mother as if she were about to prophesy.

"It was your father," said Mrs. Fairfield. "Ringing from Japan. He had an impulse to ring about an hour ago . . . and he did ring. He's coming home for a while . . . not moving in with us or anything . . . well, not yet, anyway. But he wants to see us all. He's *longing* to see us all. That's what he said . . . longing to see us. He said he was sorry that . . . he said . . . but never mind all that. It's our business—his and mine, I mean. The thing is, he asked if he could come home. And I said we'd be . . . be interested to meet him again!"

"Well," Roland said, and fell silent. "That's true! And great! That's great, Mum."

"We don't have to rush into anything," said Mrs. Fairfield. "We'll be careful."

Careful! echoed that voice in Roland's head. But this time the speaker seemed to be laughing.

"Right!" Roland said back to it. "Careful!" he said aloud, smiling at his mother. "Real life's like that, isn't it? No promises, not yet! We'll just take good care of one another and see how we go."

About the Author

MARGARET MAHY is the author of numerous picture books and middle-grade and young adult novels. She is best known for her novels, which include *24 Hours,* a winner of the Esther Glen Award; *The Tricksters,* a *New York Times* Notable Book; *Memory,* a *Boston Globe–Horn Book* Honor Book; and *The Haunting* and *The Changeover,* both Carnegie Medal winners. Ms. Mahy lives in New Zealand.

jF
Mahy, Margaret
Alchemy

Discarded by
Westfield Washington
Public Library

WESTFIELD PUBLIC LIBRARY
333 W. HOOVER ST.
WESTFIELD, IN 46074

DEMCO